UNTIL DEATH
DO US PART

UNTIL DEATH DO US PART

MARY McMULLEN

PUBLISHED FOR THE CRIME CLUB BY
DOUBLEDAY & COMPANY, INC.
GARDEN CITY, NEW YORK
1982

All of the characters in this book
are fictitious, and any resemblance
to actual persons, living or dead,
is purely coincidental.

Library of Congress Cataloging in Publication Data

McMullen, Mary, 1920–
Until death do us part.

I. Title.
PS3563.A31898U5   1982   813'.54
ISBN 0-385-18295-3
Library of Congress Catalog Card Number 82-45398

UNTIL DEATH
DO US PART

CHAPTER 1

"No!" said Jane Frame, replacing the telephone receiver with a furious crash.

"No."

She slammed the flat of her hand on the surface of her desk and was hardly aware of the stung and flaming palm.

Getting up from the desk, she stalked to the long mirror on the wall directly across from it, as though to make sure this *was* Jane Frame here before her, in Jane Frame's office in Jane Frame's large beautiful brownstone house on East Seventy-third Street. Jane Frame, who was invariably right about the really big, important things.

"No!" A shout, now. Self-control tossed aside.

A verbal hair-tearing.

It was a mild golden day in early October and one of the french windows looking out on the garden was six inches open.

Nick Quinn, planting white grape hyacinth bulbs in the far corner, under the Japanese quince, paused for a moment, raised his eyebrows to himself, and then peacefully dug another hole. He had found an apple-corer in a kitchen drawer, just right for the little bulbs.

"Oh dear," Midge Teller, Jane's assistant, said to Dana Reeves, secretary and receptionist at Jane Frame, Incorporated. They were having a mid-morning cup of coffee in Midge's office. "What on earth?"

"I have no idea. But," Dana added consideringly, "three no's ought to do it. Otherwise go next door and get Doctor

Tanager. I'm told he's very good at nervous collapses. Although I can't imagine Jane collapsing under any circumstances. What it sounds like to me is that somebody ought to get—as fast as possible—out of her way."

The Belding Group was composed of eight companies.

Corporate deliberations upon appointing a new president and general executive officer of the Group had occupied a month and a half.

"Walker North's a shoo-in," Anthony Nocella, president of Nocella Foods, had told Jane.

"Oh, Walker, of course, got to be Walker," said a vice-president of Redoubté Cosmetics and Fragrances.

"Some mention Cowan," another of her contacts, at Erax, Computers and Business Machines, had offered. Cowan was president of Erax. Naturally the man was backing his chief.

"Nonsense," Jane said.

It wasn't merely the fact that Walker North was at present her lover. She thought of him in a sense as her creation. She had plucked him, four years ago, from the vine at Squibb, where there were quite a lot of good men traffic-jamming his upward path. And placed him as a vice-president at Greave Pharmaceuticals, where there was no one ahead of him on the path but poor doddering Greave himself. A year after he joined the firm, Walker North became president of it.

Only last night, over bedroom brandy at eleven o'clock, she had said to Walker, "Well, tomorrow's your day, darling."

"Let's hope so. I keep hearing Cowan." Walker, always a high-strung, taut-wire man, got up to poke the fire and with his slashing gesture destroyed what had been a nice leaping core. He scowled at the empty brass log scoop on the hearth. "I suppose it's too late to get that houseman of yours, or whatever he is, to bring up another armload. Yes. Cowan. Cowan. His grace Malcolm Cowan."

"No. His grace Walker North."

He gave her a sharp look, his eyes narrowed. "One of the terrifying things about you, Jane—dear—is your sublime conviction that what you want to happen will of course happen. And I must say it usually does. But you know, your preference for me, for the job, might have a touch of personal bias to it."

"I never allow the personal to influence me in the slightest. Pour us another brandy and then let us, to bed."

It was seven years ago, in this same bedroom, that her marriage had ended.

In response, in the morning, to a suggestion of hers about the tie he was knotting in front of the mirror ("Not that awful magenta, it goes all too well with your eyes after a late night out") he had paused, and then said over his shoulder, "You know, Jane, I can't stand you. Never could, now that I think of it."

"Is it the Marsham woman?" Jane asked. "Or have you gone on to someone else?"

"Actually it's the Frame woman," Malcolm Cowan said in a voice of quiet ice. "Nine years with her is about eight years and eleven months too many."

Not a lengthy exchange; but a final one.

To Jane, the idea of any contemptuously rejecting human being in her immediate vicinity was unthinkable.

She watched with a face still as marble while he packed the largest of his suitcases with his most cherished clothes. "No doubt you will seize the first opportunity to throw everything else of mine out the moment the door closes behind me. I'll be at the Knickerbocker Club when Hatton wants to get in touch." Amos Hatton was their lawyer.

The divorce caused few ripples among their friends. After all, doesn't nearly everybody? was the general reaction. "Too strong for each other," said a friend of Cowan's. "Couple of bulls penned up together. Against nature." "And," amended a friend of Jane's, "he doesn't need her money anymore, with his salary and his prospects."

They had met at their mutual place of business, Bodenheim Enterprises, an untidy but wealthy conglomerate, which was the label in use before the British came up with the less intimidating and more elegant word "group."

After Vassar, from which she graduated a lonely, brilliant *summa cum laude*, Jane spent two years touring the world. There was no pressing necessity to go to work because she had inherited a great deal of Frame money from her parents, who died in the crash of a private jet when she was twenty. They had married late, and her pretty, fluttery mother was in her forties when Jane was born. "Which I imagine accounts," Jane said, and not at all in jest, "for my grown-up brain when my contemporaries were tots." Examining her when she was sixteen, her mother, Angela, née Hichens, had sighed and said, "Poor darling, all Frame and no Hichens. As you won't be pretty you might as well settle for being clever. All the Frames are very clever."

Her father, who hadn't needed a salary either, was a professor of philosophy at Harvard until at fifty he retired in delicate health to the eighty-acre Frame place in Dutchess County, New York.

Jane did go to work, though, somewhat in the manner of an obscure horse of very special breeding deciding to test its bone and muscle at steeplechase hurdles. She started as a secretary at Bodenheim Enterprises, having taught herself flawless shorthand and typing in two weeks. Up fast, up and up. When at twenty-nine she met Malcolm Cowan, she was Executive Vice-President, Personnel, of Four-Star International Inns, Bodenheim's big-money linchpin.

Nice job, took her everywhere, no problem about everywhere as she spoke four languages fluently. Powerful job, careers, or put it more plainly, lives, to make or break.

Cowan was a fellow vice-president, Pursloe Communications Systems, thirty, unmarried, in no great hurry about it because he knew he could pick and choose. He chose Jane a month after he met her. "Capable woman," he said (perhaps an odd way to describe a bride). "Marvelous brain."

"Loaded woman," corrected his friends behind his back.

During their wedding trip to Barbados, Jane's ancient maiden aunt died and left Jane all her money and worldly possessions, including the great brownstone house on Seventy-third Street. Jane left her job and redecorated the house from top to bottom. For three years—which when looked back on seemed an eternity—she played the role of wife, entertaining splendidly and being seen with her husband at all the right places at the right times. Then, bored, she went back to Bodenheim, where she was given a company to run pretty much on her own: Facades, Inc., dealing in multinational business and private real estate.

It was she who, through a client interested in buying a ranch in Argentina where he would fly weekends by Lear jet to see how his beef was coming along, found Cowan his job as executive vice-president of Erax. "The Belding Group is *the* place to be, darling," she had said. "Ceiling unlimited in every way."

After the divorce, she felt an immense need to assert herself yet again. Why hand your brains and talents over to other people? She called in a medal-winning firm of architects for ground-floor remodeling of the brownstone and founded Jane Frame, Inc. Her opening ad in *The Wall Street Journal* and *Barron's*—not in the classified section but on a quarter-page up front, her own handwriting reproduced—said, "If you consider yourself the top man in your field, your resumé belongs in my extremely active files. Jane Frame, Inc." No mention of whether you were or were not at present employed.

She ran the ad only once again, two months later; after

that she was so busy, so successfully busy, that there was no need for further advertisement of her firm.

After the *no's* ceased, there was a silence behind the slightly open door of Jane's office which Midge found unnerving.

Was Jane all right? Could she have been shouting at some sudden bodily manifestation, heart, or the first signals of a developing ulcer?

Dutiful but reluctant, she got up from her desk. She knocked lightly on the door and put her head in. Jane was standing perfectly still in front of her long mirror. There was nothing in her reflection to be read and interpreted.

She was forty-six but didn't look it. Tall, with a strong solid build. Her mother's "Poor darling, all Frame," referred to the inherited broad, flat-cheekboned face, piercing pale gray eyes under straight heavy eyebrows, oversized forehead, and firm mouth without vulnerability or tenderness to the lip. Her hair was auburn, worn in a style unchanged since her twenties, short, side-parted, flipping up a little at the ends.

There was a quality of agelessness about her which had nothing to do with beauty: her face was not expressive of her emotions but was immobile. Therefore, no register, or autobiography, of lines and dents, of mirth, discovery, sorrow, joy, or pain written upon the remembering flesh.

"I just—" Midge began. I just what? Wondered if you'd suddenly gone round the bend, in here. Or was it merely some female silliness—although one never connected female silliness with Jane—about a run showing itself on her nyloned leg, or a broken fingernail?

She spotted Nick Quinn at the far end of the garden. "Oh. Were you calling to him about where, or where *not*, to plant his bulbs?"

Not turning her head, Jane said to the mirror, "I just got a call as promised from Darius Belding, about the meeting last night. The press release will be dated as of tomorrow, so, silence please. Walker North didn't after all get the job. Malcolm Cowan did."

Funny formal way of referring to one's ex-husband. But then, now that she thought of it, Midge had not heard his name uttered by these firm lips for a number of years.

CHAPTER 2

Jane felt no personal loss of face in informing Midge of this unspeakable news.

She had chosen Midge Teller two weeks after she had opened her agency. They were old acquaintances from their early Bodenheim days, where at the time Jane zeroed in upon her and snatched her away, Midge was still in a modest-to-good job with Pursloe Communications. Jane wanted help, and efficiency; but she did not want competition, another female or male with great flair trying to prove something to *her*.

Midge was, in her quiet unobtrusive way, a perfect marvel of efficiency. "My dear wren," Jane sometimes called her to her face. "My dogsbody," she had been heard to describe her behind her back. Someone informed Midge of this term and, with a general idea of the contemptuous implications of the word, she looked it up in the Oxford English Dictionary. "A drudge, a junior person to whom a variety of menial tasks is given, a general utility person."

Now forty-three, she was short and thin with a small pointed face. "Wren" was not inaccurate, to describe the dun-brown soft hair and clear fresh brown eyes. Her mouth was pleasantly wistful and responsive. Her voice had a suggestion of a chirp to it. She had married at twenty-three and two years later her husband had left her for another woman; she had not remarried since. Her outward manner was that of cheerfulness, patience, and good temper.

Jane from the start deputed her to handle the lesser jobs that came through the office, mostly undertaken as a favor to those clients in more important positions. An executive secretary here, a department store buyer or merchandise manager there, a bookkeeper, a construction superintendent, a food broker—such was Midge's province.

She had, when Jane first knew her at Bodenheim, been Malcolm Cowan's secretary. Then, and now, and always in between, she had held and hugged to herself a silent adoring love for Malcolm Cowan.

There was a faint flush of surprise and pleasure under her fading summer crop of fine small freckles. She felt it, put a protective hand to her lower face, and said, "Oh dear, I know you did want it for Walker North."

"*Want it!*" Jane's hands, not as controllable as her face, made fists at her sides. Her eyes were obsessively on her desk telephone. "I suppose any minute now he'll be— Christ, what am I going to say to him?"

That you guessed wrong, that you goofed, Midge thought. But these words were not a part of Jane's personal vocabulary. The phone signal from the outer office made a gentle sound at the desk.

It wasn't Walker on the line. It was Dana, wanting Midge. "Your ten-thirty appointment is here, Miss Teller." When a few years back the *Times* of London had banished from its pages the use of the term "ms," Jane Frame, Inc. had immediately followed suit. Midge had returned to her maiden name when her husband left her.

Jane sat down again at her desk and thought about calling Walker. This waiting was making her feel hypertense. But no, probably he wouldn't call her, wouldn't complain, wouldn't explode; or not right away.

He wouldn't want to display the wound until it was bandaged, clean, and decent.

Walker was a proud man and not, in Jane's view, without reason. There had been Norths in government, diplomacy, law, banking, education, and medicine since George Washington was elected President of the United States. Walker's cachet in the gloves-off arena of big business was his air of family, his inherited right to place and position. He not only projected this from his own inner conviction of his patrician worth; he looked it from the outside. A chiseled young forty-five, taut, thin, his tailoring elegant but understated, his body even in repose suggesting a nervous fine-edged, directed speed. The next president of the Belding Group. Almost.

Almost, except, she thought, for bloody Cowan. Cowan, rudely descended from working Scottish railroading people. His grandfather had been an engine driver on the Flying Scot. His father, emigrating to America in his teens, had through family connections in New York gotten himself into West Point and become a career army officer. He had died on the beach of Anzio in the Second World War.

A peculiar exhaustion moved over her.

Normally she was brisk and fully functioning in the mornings. Afternoons, in the top brackets of the personnel business, were not as a rule very busy. If you were going to fire a man, you usually did it first thing in the business day. Similarly, if you were looking for a job you wanted to appear at your shaved and showered best (there were very few beards, although many mustaches, among Jane's five- and six-figure job-seekers).

She buzzed Dana. "No calls, nothing, for the rest of the morning," she said. "Please tell Nick I'll want a dozen oysters and a carafe of Chablis for my lunch. At one."

She went out one of the two doors of her office, into the house's main entrance hall, took the deliberately antique little elevator, a wrought-iron cage, to the third floor, got out, and went in a numbed way to her bedroom. She lay down on her bed and drew her own mental curtains.

Silence, darkness, unconsciousness. Blessed zero.

It wasn't all that pressing, as it was only twenty of eleven, but Dana went out into the garden to deliver Jane's lunch order to Nick Quinn.

The sun and light became her. She looked, Nick thought, and not for the first time, like Somebody's Portrait of Someone; but both without a name to latch onto. Face of adventurous aquiline bones, loose chestnut hair in a toss of natural ringlets, widely set violet eyes. Tall and graceful, but relaxed and at home with herself. Wherever she was, indoors or out, there was a sense of pipers' tunes in the distance and fresh meadow winds blowing on her careless hair.

He palmed soil over the last of his two dozen grape hyacinths and got up from his kneeling position. He gazed at her with interest.

"I suppose it's part of your job to be good looking," he said, not in flattery but as the fruit of something mulled over.

"Yes," Dana said. "Every morning, when I get up, I put on my features to take along to work. After my shower, that is."

This lively answer had something of a challenge in it.

What he was really saying, it seemed to her, was: What on earth are you doing in a mindless job when you look like a girl who could do anything?

They had only known each other for three weeks but already there was a reading of minds beginning between them.

I am a secretary-receptionist, Dana explained to herself, because I have no special gifts or talents and I am not interested in the bare-knuckled blood-letting task of getting ahead, as a woman, in some significant profession. This was in its way a colorful and often dramatic method of spending the day and turning an honest dollar—watching the Jane Frame scene. Dukes, earls, knights, princes of the American business establishment, to-ing and fro-ing on the telephone and in person.

Her salary was excellent. She thought she might slip gradually into personnel work herself; that is, if she didn't decide at some point to devote herself to enjoying a man full time. In the meantime she found life very pleasant.

And, looking at him standing in the sunlight, she thought, here's the pot calling the kettle black. Nicholas Quinn, live-in maintenance man. In charge of the garden, cooking, office cleanup after hours, setting out of trash and garbage, floor waxing, window washing, painting, and carpentering when needed.

What are *you* all about?

Jane had merely said, "You have a good eye, Dana. He's hired," and to Midge, "There will be a man moving in tomorrow. For good, I hope."

The neighborhood was high in burglaries. Expensive locking devices were all very well; but burglars sufficiently determined had taken to removing entire doors or windows. "The police are too busy to take constant care of us little people," Jane added, with an ironic curve of her upper lip. "Little people" indeed. *Jane Frame.* "I thought a man would be better than a guard dog, or two guard dogs. After all, he doesn't have to be walked. He has his own sanitary facilities in the basement."

Now, "A dozen oysters for madam's lunch," Dana said to Nick. "If I recall correctly, she likes fresh lemon wedges but no red goo to dip them into. I see the parsley is doing nicely, you might add a touch of that. I think she meant the half-carafe, not the large one."

Nick smiled at her, an easy-going good-humored smile which did not open his lips. "And, for you, Dana? Or are you eating out?"

"Yes. Do you really like to cook? I thought"—she smiled back at him—"that not to be impolite and prying I would ask you one question a week and then in say three months satisfy my curiosity about you."

"I do like to cook. You're aware that the gender of the

word chef is masculine. What was Jane Frame shouting 'no' about?"

"Her favorite horse didn't win the Derby. The wreath of roses is around the neck of her ex-husband, a man named Cowan."

"Malcolm Cowan. Yes, I've heard of him."

"Another puzzle-piece fitted in. You must have had something to do with business."

"I did. You have no idea what a relief it is to wax a parquet floor on a nice morning, which is my next immediate project."

Turning to go back into the house, Dana said, "Happy waxing to you, Nicholas Quinn. Middle name?"

Face bland, he answered, "Montmorency."

It was after seven when Walker North called.

Jane was sitting alone in her living room. There were no lights on and the room was dim, illumined only, in a ghostly way here and there, by the polished sheen of an inlaid card table near a window, the apricot gleam of Scalamandré damask on a loveseat. The tall double doors into the hall were open. For some reason she felt a need of being in touch; but there was nobody here to be in touch with except Midge, whose typewriter could be heard distantly.

A great many of Midge's people had to make appointments with her during their lunchtime or after work. Tonight, she had told Jane, she was expecting an advertising agency art director who had been sure of getting the job as head art director and had been edged out by another man.

Then she added in a tongue-biting manner, "Oh. I'm sorry, Jane, I'd forgotten for a moment that . . ."

"Pity you have to be kept here till all hours while he no doubt fortifies himself for his interview with three martinis," Jane said. And went on, with chilling tactless truth, "But then there's nobody at home waiting for you to cook dinner."

She let the telephone, the number of which was unlisted

and was on a different line from the office, ring three times before she got up and answered it.

Don't give any impression that you were waiting close by to snatch up the receiver. Whoever it was at the other end.

"Evening, Jane," Walker said, voice calm. "I called to say a quick good-bye."

"Good-bye? What *can* you mean?"

"I have to leave tonight for São Paulo. The manager of R and D in our installation there has gone berserk and is terrorizing the office. Unfortunately he's in the possession of some top-secret stuff."

"Oh, too bad, good luck." It was eerie that he hadn't mentioned Cowan. Of course he would know by now. Everybody would know by now.

She thought it would have been easier to deal with an outpouring of rage than this cool ignoring of the subject. She wondered if it was true, about the crisis in São Paulo. And if it was true, didn't he have other executives on hand to deal with berserk Research and Development managers?

Or was he just running away . . . from the first 21-gun crash of the news echoing throughout the business world, and the directors' dinners, and the handshakes, and the congratulations waiting for Cowan.

Don't let him run away.

Refuse to play his nothing's-happened-at-all game.

"Darling, about Cowan . . ." Now, Walker, take it from there.

He did. "Oh, Cowan. Could it be that you're losing your grip, old girl?" Light, amused, an icy coldness underneath. "It turns out I was right all along. One in the eye for the infallible Jane Frame. I imagine we'll both recover from it, in our own separate ways."

Separate ways.

Good-bye.

She was by no means ready to file and forget her emotional

need and physical passion for Walker; they'd only started this thing five weeks ago and it had turned out to be rather marvelous.

"We'll talk when you get back," she said, a little unsteadily, a little humbly, not sounding to herself like herself.

"If our chap has to be dumped—or more probably stashed under observation in our own infirmary so he doesn't go running off to Lambert or Squibb with his loaded pieces of paper —his replacement will be in your hands. Little silver linings, you know. As my good-bye seems to have unmanned you, good night then, Jane. Dear."

His replacement. Silver linings to unnamed disasters.

A stinging slap across her face.

CHAPTER 3

Malcolm Cowan formally assumed the presidency of the Belding Group on a Monday.

Three days later he fired Walker North.

Cowan seldom asked for his second wife's advice but often found her useful as a sounding board, a way to make his own thoughts known to him out loud, thus firming them.

They were dressing for the black-tie directors' dinner. Cowan was perfectly capable of managing his own bow tie but Agatha liked to do it for him. It reminded her, she said, of happy couples in old movies. She was five years older than he was and recalled Myrna Loy applying herself to William Powell's black tie.

"I imagine," he said, standing patiently, chin up, "that North is not a happy man. Some people thought it was neck and neck, but of course I never did."

"I imagine," Agatha agreed placidly, "that he would like to see you drawn and quartered as thousands cheer."

Walker North was not present at the directors' dinner; the only one of the eight Belding company presidents in absentia.

On Tuesday night Cowan was guest of honor at a cocktail party given jointly by Belding members Lynas Aircraft and Redoubté Cosmetics and Fragrances.

The second-in-command at Lynas had worked for Cowan at Erax several years back and was decidedly his man. After a number of drinks, he beckoned Cowan into a corner, and told him, with a combination of loyalty, indiscretion, and the sound idea of advancing himself anew in Cowan's regard, that it might be wise to keep an eye on Walker North. Particularly in connection with his guardianship of Greave Pharmaceuticals.

Walker, he said, had, upon hearing of the choice of Cowan late last week, muttered to someone who whispered it to someone else who passed it along to him, Bellows of Lynas, that Walker might be contemplating pulling Greave out of Belding and starting his own group. Anthony Nocella of Nocella Foods, he added, had been very high on Walker North and might conceivably join the dissident.

"Ah," Cowan said. He had made this syllable very much his own. He found it more useful than the blank or questioning "Oh." It could be crisp and brief, as now; or it could be drawn out to suggest depth under depth of meaning. "Thanks, Joe. I'll tuck it away in an inside pocket. Wasn't Walker invited to this party?"

"Yes, but he's away somewhere, Brazil or somewhere."

Belding Towers was on East Fifty-fourth Street, a simple fifty-story limestone shaft with a slender wing set back at one side and a broad fountained terrace in front of the wing.

Belding occupied three quarters of the building. Cowan's offices were on the top floor, reached by a private express elevator as well as being accessible by the main elevators. The Group's various corporate members were spread here and there on four continents but each had a central office and staff on Fifty-fourth Street. And each was under the eye there, and answerable to, Malcolm Cowan.

It was the policy of the directors of the Group to give its head man not only a great deal of power but a sweeping freedom to exercise it. Otherwise, how to keep all these important and ambitious men, and all this money, in line?

Cowan thought it would be wise to take Walker North's pulse in person as early in the game as possible. What would be the future attitude, face-to-face, of this near-winning loser? He thought he knew, but go ahead, prove it.

He instructed his executive secretary, Anne Pence, to get hold of Walker North for him at the earliest opportunity.

Just to cover himself—in case his instincts were correct—he had a few words with Kellyng, the board chairman. "Gracious!" Kellyng said. He was a Quaker and had never been heard to use strong language. "Well, you ought to be the man to know the board trusts your judgment, Mal."

On Thursday morning at ten o'clock, Anne conducted Walker into the 70-by-50-foot quarters of Cowan, divided by sliding glass doors into two rooms, one a sumptuously comfortable living room, one the office proper.

Cowan chose to be found at his desk, which was large, black, gleaming, and fashionably bare. He rose and held out a hand.

"Good morning, Walker."

He was pleased to sense the buttoned-down, held-in rage of the other man, the only sign being an odd white tightness about the finely carved nostrils.

"My first chance to see how you would become the throne room, or vice versa," Walker said. He allowed himself an examination of Cowan that came within a hairline of being insolent.

Cowan was in his late forties, of medium height, heavy-shouldered and fit. He was a strikingly handsome man. Heavy inverted V's of eyebrows over large brilliant gray eyes, firm strong-willed mouth, dramatic cheekbones above deep lower dents that were masculine first cousins to dimples. His hair was gray-brown and thick and barbered with authority. His manner was as secretly contained as a cat's, in sharp contrast to his projection of male and almost military power. His clothing was as good and as expensive as Walker's but more, agreeably, visible.

("He's not that much smarter than some of the rest of us,"

Sigismund Lynas of Lynas Aircraft said when he heard the news. "It's just his way of—no other word for it—mesmerizing people. Taking over a room. Looking like the only one in it. He'll come in very handy when the next committee in Washington calls us in to talk about cost overruns.")

He sat perfectly still under Walker's gaze. He said in his deep easy voice, "Too bad you missed all the fun—the crowning, as it were, if we're to continue with your analogy of the throne room. You were"—he looked down at his hands and his cheek-dents deepened—"very much missed."

Against his will, Walker offered an explanation but made it purposely inadequate.

"A to-do in São Paulo. Sorry. But then, champagne is not one of my favorite beverages."

"Still, your absence made a conspicuous, if not aching, void."

"Should I have brought a letter from my mother here with me to tell the principal why I had to skip class?" Walker startled himself by the open fury that rushed up and boiled over.

"No, but you might have brought a word of congratulation with you," Cowan said mildly. "Even though . . ."

That did it. Walker had no idea later what things he said to Cowan, what a pour of terrible things. Ending up shouting, two minutes—three minutes—five minutes later?

The office was soundproofed but underneath the desk the recording equipment was as always in operation. Most but not all of the big men in Belding knew about the hidden ear.

Walker, listening now to his own and Cowan's silence, knew about it. What did it matter now, what did anything matter?

Cowan looked at his watch. "Ten-ten. Let's call this a parting by mutual agreement. I think our associates will understand. From my own point of view, here, as everywhere, hurt feelings are a bore to have around and are literally counterproductive. You know our rules. Off any and all Belding

Group premises immediately, and that will be say ten-eleven. A year's salary to be paid to you within one month. Your other equities in the Group will be studied by our lawyers and made good within six months."

He got up from his desk but did not offer his hand.

Walker turned, went to the door, opened it, and stopped at Anne Pence's desk in her glass-walled office outside Cowan's.

"I always forget where the express elevator is hidden away," he said. "I haven't used it that often. Will you lead me to it? It happens that I am in rather a hurry."

She later told her assistant secretaries that she would never forget the smile on his face.

CHAPTER 4

"Do you own a gun?"

It was nine-thirty on Thursday morning. Nick Quinn was busy washing the french windows of Jane's sitting room. He was working on the outside, standing on the black-painted wrought-iron balcony. The windows were open aslant. She had come upstairs for her gold pencil, which she thought she had left on the table near the window.

"No." He cast an eye upward, to the gray sky. "I remember an aunt or my mother saying that when you wash the windows it always rains the next day. My timing seems to be shaping up well for that."

Single-minded, Jane found her pencil marking her place in the book she had been reading, *Third World: Expansion Opportunities in the Raw.* "My aunt always kept one on her bedside table. A gun, I mean. Very small, old-fashioned, inlaid, and all that nonsense, but I suppose it works. I think you'd better have it. It's in the safe. I'll get it out while I think of it."

The windowpanes were too small to allow the use of a squeegee. Nick cleared one of them to brilliance with a balled-up page of the New York *Times.*

"I don't know about that," he objected. "Your ad didn't say anything about a trained gunman. Which I am not."

"A man of your obvious mental capacities," Jane said, "should have no great difficulty in grasping the principle of pointing at a target and pulling a trigger. Only in dire emergency, of course. I'll put it in the drawer of *your* bedside

table. Along with ammunition—she kept a good big box of
that. I don't suppose it goes stale?"

The ad, set in display type in the Help Wanted columns,
had said, "General utility and maintenance man for large private New York town house. Must live in. Comfortable quarters w. own bath. If applicant can cook, generous salary will
be upped by ⅓. No bedmaking, dishwashing, etc. involved as
daily cleaning persons handle domestic matters. Call only
betw. 9–12, 2–5 o'clock."

"You'll get a bundle of off-the-street horrors," Jane told
Dana, who was to be in charge of screening. "I only want to
see, myself, anyone who in your judgment is absolutely all
right. Tell everyone else the position is filled. You can't put
this in an ad these days, but I would like someone reasonably
young and reasonably strong, as what I want is a house guard-
ian of sorts. And—you know, of course—someone you
wouldn't be afraid to be alone in the house *with*."

Tall order, said Dana to herself.

"Conduct any and all interviews in the basement office. I
don't want these gentry sprawling about my reception room."

The classified ad had been clipped and delivered to Nick as
a form of joke by his friend Coleman Hays the morning after
they spent a long late night drinking together. A messenger
from the Boniface Bank brought the envelope while he was
having his breakfast.

In the course of the festivities (Coley just back from a year
in his bank's Amsterdam branch) Nick had addressed his
friend solemnly. He said he didn't know *what* the hell he was
doing in corporation law, and that he was at a personal cross-
roads, and was wasting his life, and was tempted to say the
hell with corporation law and Giddings, Mortimer and
Quinn. And a good deal more of the same. Coley listened
with sympathy and said if there was anything worse than corporation law it was investment banking. "But what would

you do if you just up and walked away from it? How would you live in the style to which you are so well accustomed?"

"I don't know—write a book, or a play. I've always wanted to try a play."

"That's your old grandmother coming out in you." Nick's maternal grandmother had been the once legendary and now forgotten Russian actress Anna Verdanska.

"Her genes," said Nick, "must be stirring in my veins. Or do you suppose it's only the whiskey? But I've been feeling this way for months."

Usually the rude bright morning dispenses with, or corrects, the night flights of fancy. This medicine, often bitter to swallow, did not effect its cure now.

Two teasing, and tantalizing, and delightful words floated to the forefront of Nick's brain.

Why not?

Room and board. Honest toil. He could cook, and cook well. Up goes the salary by one third. His own quarters w. bath. Was the job already taken? Coley had noted in pencil the date of the ad: yesterday.

Was it all too good to be true? In this city, with its many little pockets of madness, was it perhaps some nut, female, advertising for a live-in lover?

There was only one way to find out.

He seldom arrived at work before ten, a matter about which his uncle Sergius Quinn chided him gently once every six months. "It's not that it affects your own work, you're uncommonly fast and good, dear boy, but it does set a bad example for the staff."

I didn't, Nick often reminded himself, even climb upward in the cherished American way, rung by sweating rung. His uncle had started him on the fifth or sixth rung up when he got out of law school.

At several minutes past nine, he called the number given in the clipping. A charming voice gave him an appointment at

ten, and the house address. "Go down the basement steps
behind the front rail and ring the bell."

How did you dress to convey the impression of being a
good, reliable utility and maintenance man? It was early Sep-
tember and a clean brown-and-white striped seersucker suit
ought to be taken as neat but not gaudy. With the phrase
"blue-collar" leaping to mind, a pale blue shirt and plain
brown knitted tie. Sneakers, perhaps, to suggest agility and
readiness to work. And certainly do not arrive in front of the
house by taxi. He had time enough to walk the distance; his
apartment was on West End Avenue near Lincoln Center.

There was a moment of slight confusion when after ringing
the bell he was admitted at the basement door by a remarkably good-looking girl.

"The reception room is upstairs, on the parlor floor," she
said.

Reception room of what? Was this not after all a private
house as the ad had stated, or was it a company of some kind?

"But you said the basement. At least I think it was you."

Her eyebrows rose. "*I* said the basement?"

"On the telephone, to me, just after nine. My name is
Quinn." Don't say Nicholas, too fancy for menial work.
"Nick Quinn."

"Oh. Well then, come into the office." A small room in
which, he thought, in palmier well-servanted days the housekeeper might have seen to the ordering of her household
books.

He had no intention of telling all, to this girl; she might
very well conclude that he was of unsound mind, wanting to
dump a highly salaried position in a Wall Street law firm for
this job.

In the course of the short interview, he said he was tired of
desk work and wanted a change.

Dana was of a resilient nature. He was somewhat of a mystery, but on the other hand he was a welcome near-impos-

sibility and an astonishing prize. She had interviewed eleven men yesterday, finding Jane's forecast correct. One of them had tried, drunkenly, to embrace her.

But, this man? Well, it was a different world now. People felt free to choose the way they wished to live. And a good thing too. Especially in view of the style of applicant she had been expecting to repeat itself all day.

"I suppose you can supply some kind of references from your last job?"

Yes, he could. (He would have his secretary, an obliging girl, write a letter stating that he was a man of good character and regular work habits.)

Let Jane take it from here, Dana thought. But don't, in the meantime, hand him forms to fill out. He might get bored, or impatient, and walk away. Or evaporate into air.

Two minutes later she ushered him into Jane's office and left them together.

Jane, her face expressing no surprise whatever at this candidate for her job, explained briefly what his duties would be. Then, "I don't suppose I should look a gift horse in the mouth, but I must. You're a man of education and what is known as background. What *are* you doing here?"

Having leapt the first hurdle, in the basement, he thought he could be more forthcoming with her. He had felt for some months, years even, that he wanted to write, or try to, and that it occurred to him it was now or never. He hadn't the time in his law job. This, he added, must be strictly between them; if he did fall on his face, he didn't want to have to go around explaining the fiasco to all the world.

His explanation made sense to Jane, who was a great believer in doing exactly what one wants to do. "But if, say in six months, you come up with a best-selling book or successful play, what then? I will have to require you to sign a contract for one year. Terminable of course on my side if your work is not done to my satisfaction, or if you turn out to drink to excess. Or"—she was not a woman given to smiling often but she smiled now—"if your cooking is perfectly awful. The salary will be ten thousand a year. Two nights off, when I will arrange for another security man. When can you start?"

"Give me a week." Rufus Brown, the man on the rung directly under his, would be more than capable and very much delighted at taking over.

His Uncle Sergius was surprised but not unduly disturbed. "Did I ever tell you, dear boy, that in my late twenties I left my job—of course I wasn't married then, but neither are you —and went off to Italy to paint? I turned out to be awful at it, but I enjoyed myself immensely. I don't think we'll accept your formal resignation, but you may take an unlimited leave of absence, and more power to you."

His apartment lease had two months to run. Coley, who hadn't yet found a place of his own and was living at the Yale Club, happily agreed to take it over. "What will I tell everybody?" he asked. "That you've flipped?"

"No, I'll handle any friendly inquiries as they crop up. Don't tell anybody anything for the time being."

"I think I envy you," Coley said. "Damn it, why didn't I apply myself?"

When Nick had finished the sitting room windows he went down to his basement abode, a large if low-ceilinged living-bedroom arrangement. His typewriter was set on a table which got light from a high-set, heavily barred window. The feeling was not that of a jail, but of heady freedom.

He went to the lamp table beside the big comfortable double bed and opened the drawer. The little gun was there, with its box of ammunition. Jane Frame was not a woman to say she was going to do something and then forget all about it.

He composed mentally his next order from his employer.

"Take that gun, Nick, see that it's loaded, and go shoot Malcolm Cowan through the heart."

CHAPTER 5

After having closed the lamp table drawer on the gun, Jane stood gazing about her. She had never before entered Nick's quarters. As she was here, she was not now—or ever—inclined to let fastidious manners stand in the way of curiosity. Knowing about people, getting the feel of them, discovering things they might want left unknown put power in your hands.

The room was clean and tidy, the bed made, but then he didn't do it himself. Two women, one black, one white, came in every day except Sunday, Mrs. Phillips from nine until three and Ethel Hammer from three until nine.

She opened his closet and found without surprise the labels she would have expected in the scant collection of clothes he kept. Good clothes, even though he'd probably chosen from his wardrobe the ones that weren't new. Brooks Brothers. Lord and Taylor. His bureau drawers weren't particularly orderly. Nothing fancy in the way of shirts, but, L. L. Bean, Maine, on a collar label. Austin Reed, Regent Street. Bloomingdale's. Brooks Brothers again.

No surreptitious collection of empty liquor bottles.

She lifted the cover on his typewriter, an Olivetti electric portable, Praxis 48 model. There was a sheet of manila paper in it, a good deal of X-ing out to be seen.

"Dana enters and walks to the fireplace, where she angrily kicks a log." Stage directions. Dana? Well, one imagined that when a writer was roughing out something he might seize the first names that were handy.

There were no photographs to be seen. Dear old mother in

a silver frame—although if he was thirty-one she needn't be that old. No snapshots of pretty girls tucked around the mirror over the dresser. He must have a girl, or several; he didn't come across as homosexual.

Well, enough lingering. He *was* writing something or other, he was not, from his general demeanor or any hidden evidence here, a drinker who couldn't hope to hold any other kind of job. He must have been, oddly enough, telling her the truth about himself. Which so few people did. And he was without any question an amazing stroke of luck. He cooked with imagination and authority but without fuss and frills. In every way, an admirable acquisition.

She had found the door of his room locked and let herself in with one of the fourteen house keys dangling from a brass ring. Naturally—why wouldn't he want his privacy? When she left, she pressed the little button under the inside knob that reset the lock.

Were he and Dana up to something? That nice big bed for a playground?

And if they were, what of it?

But it was good to know, useful to know, what was going on around her. Even in matters of the most minor importance.

When she returned to her office, a call from an angry man named Baker was waiting on her line.

"That job at RCA," he said. "I was interviewed this morning. When we got to salary I gave him the figure you gave me —remember, Jane? Sixty-five thousand, you said. No problem, you said, the man before you was making sixty. He all but threw me out. That is, he said, 'You're miles over our budget,' and got up and shook my hand and said he'd enjoyed meeting me anyway and that was the end of that."

Probably, Jane thought, he didn't think you were qualified. Or just didn't like you personally and took the easy obvious way out. Human chemistry, the mysterious reactions of one person to another, was an X factor you could do absolutely nothing about. Not even if you were Jane Frame.

But.

Walker's voice in her ear, "Could it be that you're losing your grip, old girl?"

Old girl. He'd never used that phrase to her before. Old. Losing your . . .

Nonsense. It was merely that she had had a bad night, only a few tossing snatches of sleep, thinking as she had been doing night after night, about Cowan, about Walker.

To Baker, she said, "Well, onward and upward. There's a man at NBC who's wobbly. I'll talk to a few people there and get back to you as soon as possible."

"Well, Jesus, I'd banked on RCA. Literally. I need something fast or I'll be thrown in debtors' prison."

With the disapproval of the independently wealthy, Jane wondered why a great many high-salaried people lived up to and often far beyond every cent they made.

The business of the day proceeded in a normal way until noon, in spite of its proprietor's persistent, slow-burning rage.

The house was, as usual, quiet. There were none of the door-spinning comings and goings, the hum of business being done, the racketing telephones ("I'll put you on hold for just a moment") one might associate with a firm dealing solely in people and taking in a very large annual income.

At no time were clients to be seen making a small crowd in the reception room; hopeful or neutral or near hopeless people, sitting waiting for their turns. Interviews were by appointment only. The interviews were widely spaced so that there would be no nervous watch checking, knee swinging, turning of magazine and newspaper pages. Although a broad low table held fresh periodicals, American and English, French, Italian, and Japanese.

The reception room was, however, a pleasant place to wait

in if you were on rare occasions forced to do so. It was a large, high-ceilinged room with three long windows facing the street. On the parquet floor was a tawny apricot-golden rug, an Oushak. The furniture was light and graceful, French and English. On one wall, a marble fireplace with a mirrored chimney breast offered comfort to the eye and soul from October until April with its wood fire. Dana's English Regency table desk was across from the fireplace, decorated not only by its occupant but always with a crystal bowl or Ming vase of fresh flowers. It was a task of Dana's, which she enjoyed, to stop each morning at the florist's three doors away and choose and then arrange the day's flowers.

Midge thought it was a shame to throw yesterday's flowers ruthlessly away so they got a second go-round in her office. It was half the size of Jane's, but in no sense a squeezed space. There was nothing to be seen of the drama and color found in Jane's office. Beige walls, simple white furniture, everything in immaculate order.

Midge was in the middle of a busy morning. At ten-thirty she got a call from a woman wanting a cook and told her politely that the firm did not handle domestic employment. Although Jane had once—to accommodate the president of Union Chemical—burgled an entire staff of servants for his new island palace in the Bahamas. A butler here, a cook there, filched from the employ of her friends and acquaintances. No one ever knew who was responsible for this simultaneous disruption of service in ten different houses and apartments.

At eleven o'clock, Midge and Dana were having coffee, freshly made on Midge's electric ring, when Nick Quinn appeared outside the window and began vigorously to wash it. Hospitable Midge crooked a finger, beckoning him, and held up her cup in illustration.

A moment later he joined them. A tall lithe man, his body suggesting civilized power. He was open-faced and broad-browed. His hair was red-fair, his eyes deeply set and remarkably blue. He brought into the room with him his air, curiously reassuring, of inner contentment, humor, and ease. His work clothes were appropriate but attractive, clean chinos, tennis sneakers, today a denim shirt which Dana knew had cost him twenty-two-fifty because she had bought the same shirt as a birthday present for her current man.

The front-door buzzer sounded as he was lifting his cup to his lips. "I'll get it," he said. "No, I will," said Dana. "It's not on your list of things to do."

She admitted a small slim girl with deliberately tousled ashy hair falling into her large golden-brown eyes.

"Yes?" Dana asked. "I don't seem to have you in my appointment book for eleven."

"I'm not here for a job, but for Nick Quinn," the girl said.

Nick appeared in Midge's doorway, still holding his cup. "I'm not allowed visitors during working hours," he told her with mild severity. "But as long as you're here I can give you ten minutes in the garden."

Immediately following this, a man called, identifying himself as Riordan of City Hall. City Hall sounding like Jane territory, Dana put through the call to her. Jane, who had been sitting motionless at her desk, answered as she always did, "Jane Frame," in her clear forthright way. Riordan wanted to know if she had anyone on her books who was an expert on the treatment and disposal of municipal waste.

"Not at the moment, but I'll cast an eye about," Jane said. She never used in any of her dealings the word "search." She thought it was both too fashionable and too commercial and also suggested an inability to come up with the right and almost immediate person for any given job.

She had no network of branch offices, relying instead on what the newspapers called informed sources. Her years with Bodenheim had provided her with national and international contacts of immense value. She very seldom had to reimburse

her inside informants, only occasionally on demand splitting
a commission. But the majority of these convenient people
were satisfied on two levels: it was nice to have a personal in
with Jane Frame, just in case; it was also nice to have been
partly responsible for the appearance on the scene of some
shining new executive.

It was one of these informants who, a little before noon,
called Jane from the Greave executive offices in the Belding
Tower. She was Sara Larme, who was now personnel head of
Greave.

"You'll never believe it, Jane," she began, and paused for
dramatic effect.

"Believe what?" Jane asked, an unaccustomed weariness in
her voice.

"Our whole floor is quivering with excitement. I had three
interviews in a row to do or I would have called you sooner.
Sometime in mid-morning they put a"—another pause—"a
padlock on Walker North's door. I just checked, the security
guard is still standing in front of the door. And you know
what that means."

Jane knew well what that meant. In many organizations,
when a person above a certain salary level was discharged he
was ordered immediately off the business premises and his
office locked against him. The theory being that in his rage he
might turn destructive, tear up or steal valuable documents,
start a fire, or in the extreme case hurl himself out of the
office window. This last not helpful to a company's image.

"What?" Her voice sounded to her flat, and pale, and far
away.

"Well, I know it's hard to believe. Of course there is only
one person who could have fired Walker out of hand, and
that's Malcolm Cowan. Flexing his muscles or something.
I'm told via grapevine that Walker had a ten o'clock appointment with Cowan. Next thing, the lock and the guard. Well,

I mean, what else to think about who pushed him off the high diving board?"

Silence.

"Jane, are you still on the line?" Sara Larme had heard about Walker's affair with Jane, which made the delivery of her thunderbolt even more fascinating.

"Yes. I'm," the literal truth, "taking it in, that's all." There could be other explanations. There must be. Of course. Of course.

"Thanks, Sara. Before we say good-bye . . ." Some iron in her character came to her aid, and did so to her surprise. "Midge told me this morning she has an awfully good girl for you, for the personnel assistant job. I suppose she couldn't reach you what with your jam-up of interviews, but you'll no doubt be hearing from her. In the meantime, take care."

She ordered her curiously emptied mind to think out the alternative possibilities.

Today was, let's see, Thursday. Walker got back from São Paulo yesterday afternoon. Perhaps he brought back with him important papers, formulas, something like that, seized from his demented man. Called to a meeting at the main Greave plant in Bridgeport, Connecticut. Tells his secretary to have his office closely guarded as he hasn't yet put the papers in the company safe. Or, having returned with damaging evidence about the man, been pursued on the next plane by some enraged Latin family member, brother, sister, wife, bent on personal revenge. For at least a week keep my office under close guard . . . The world of business, she well knew, was not immune to adventures smacking of the annals of the CIA.

She didn't even know if he had checked in at his office yesterday. He hadn't called her when he came back. Her pride fought for a while with her powerful will and lost the battle. She called his apartment at Manhattan House at ten o'clock

Wednesday night. Just at the hour at which she had called Monday night, and Tuesday night.

His voice was somewhere between sleepy and peevish. "For God's sake, Jane, I was trying to get some sleep in after that flight."

"Just saying hello, darling, then off you go back to sleep. I suppose I'll see you tomorrow?"

"I don't know. Probably not." There was neither aggression nor apology in his voice. "I may treat myself after a day's catching up to a long weekend in the country."

Walker kept the Manhattan House apartment for on-and-off use during the week. He and his wife, Candide, had a year-round house in Tarrytown.

The long weekend, possibly extending through Tuesday, was meant, Jane thought, as an announcement to the Belding Group and specifically to Cowan: I am a man of importance, and an independent man, the president of Greave Pharmaceutical. Naturally I arrange my schedule as I please.

Foolish of you, Walker. It comes off like a sulk. But she didn't say this aloud. For one thing, she hadn't time to lead up to her good advice. He said abruptly, "I must really get back to bed, I've had it. We'll be in touch."

In touch. Meaningless words she often fell back on herself.

After Sara Larme's call, after working out what really must have happened, to explain the padlock and the guard, she dialed the Manhattan House number. He might have canceled his ten o'clock appointment with Cowan. He might be sleeping late. There was no answer.

Could he have fled to the country a day early? Or, not fled, in his eyes, but shouted his declaration of independence. She could hardly call Tarrytown herself. Candide knew her, knew her voice, probably knew about her and Walker.

She dialed Midge's number. Midge wouldn't be out to

lunch until a good deal later because of her midday appointments.

"Do me a favor, Midge. Call Walker's number in Tarrytown, I'll give it to you in a moment, and whoever answers, say you're trying to contact him, where can he be reached right away? You can say who you are—no one will know the name anyway—but don't mention Jane Frame."

Midge called her back in three minutes. "I got Mrs. North. She says he's just back from São Paulo and told her he'd be tied up in meetings all day today, but if it's any kind of business emergency she's sure he can be reached at the Tower."

There was no place to hide now.

The shock wave of the truth hit head-on.

This time there was no shouting. No striding the room. No peering in the mirror to make sure it was Jane Frame looking back at her.

She felt her facial muscles firming to rock.

She was Jane Frame all right, flooded with her own identity and her own strength, exciting in her veins as brandy.

She knew what Jane Frame, now, would do.

CHAPTER 6

The ad in the classified pages of the New York *Times* was neither large nor showy. The only display type, and that was of modest size, was at the beginning:

"EXCELLENT OPPORTUNITY FOR RIGHT PERSON. Pres and gen ex officer, Belding Grp. Must have diversified exp in all phases of operation from concept through planning to marketing. Salary commensurate with abilities. All applic confidential. Contact Miss Flower at 201-752-4000."

It appeared on Friday morning.

Esther Parano was one of Anne Pence's four secretarial assistants. She had long cherished a personal dislike for Anne ("I mean, who does she think she is anyway, the Queen of Sheba?"), and entertained herself every morning at her coffee break by going ostentatiously through the classified pages. Once Anne had asked crisply, "Job hunting, Esther?" and she had smiled back in what she hoped was a secret and unsettling way. "I have five brothers, remember? and one of them's always out of work."

She almost choked on a swallow of coffee when she came upon the quiet little ad, this Friday morning. She ringed it in red pencil and marched out of the comfortable sitting room provided for their morning and afternoon breaks. She strode into Anne's office. "Lucky my brother Eddie's unemployed—again. Look at this, what I found."

Anne read it once, and then again. "But," she said in a dazed voice, "Miss Flower is Mr. Kellyng's secretary. And this is Mr. Kellyng's telephone number."

Before she was able to think rationally, or even think at all, Cowan's number button on her desk console lit up. Where had all the air gone? She drew a great breath. "Mr. Cowan's office."

Tabitha Flower said, "What in God's name is all this, Anne? I've already had three calls from men wanting to be president of the Belding Group. Even before I looked and found the ad. Is someone over there playing jokes? Mr. Kellyng left yesterday for Palm Springs, which I suppose in a way is a good thing, his heart's not all that able to cope."

"I'm going right in to see Mr. Cowan, I'll call you back," Anne said. "Of course it's a joke. He only *started* Monday of this week."

Malcolm Cowan, after the first split-second blast of white shock, was able to cope.

"Get in touch with the head of the classified section. Find out any particulars you can. People are usually billed for ads placed by phone; get the name and address of whoever called this in. Get Blaine up here immediately." Joel Blaine was the vice-president in charge of Belding public relations.

The *Times* that Friday was full of near apocalyptic news, from the Persian Gulf, from Washington, from China, but the thunderous item of the day in certain circles in New York was the little ad, one column wide by one-half an inch deep.

Lunchtime conversations at New York's better restaurants resounded with it. Over martinis, scotches, the dieting or reformed sips of Chablis, Campari and soda, Perrier water, "excellent opportunity for right person" was the prime and merrymaking topic. A man attacking his steak *au poivre* at Quo Vadis said to his companion, "How about this for Monday's classified section? 'Political person wanted. Unparalleled opportunity. Emolument suited to responsibilities of position. Use of several residences provided as well as private plane. Secret Service Protection 24 hours a day. Contact Miss Smith, 1600 Pennsylvania Avenue, Washington, D.C.' "

Dana as a favor to busy Midge went over the classified ads every morning and clipped out anything she thought might be of interest to Midge.

At about nine-thirty she came upon the excellent opportunity as next president of the Belding Group. Midge's nine o'clock interview was just leaving, a tall piratical-looking man who gave the impression of having a handy knife tucked into his belt under his suit jacket.

"He looks so Spanish Main," Midge said as Dana came into her office with her little sheaf of clippings. "And d'you know what he is? A certified public accountant."

"Midge, read this." Dana placed the top clipping on Midge's blotter. She was startled at Midge's reaction. A faint gasp, and then a raw pink flush of—what was it?—personal outrage?

"But how dreadful," Midge said, her voice unsteady. "How cruel. Who could have done such a horrible thing?"

"You don't think anyone will really take it seriously?" Dana asked. "It's so obviously a nasty joke. It's like advertising for a, I don't know, new Pope or something."

Anne found out from the *Times* that a man named McPharrie, a classified ad-taker, had received a call at about one o'clock on Thursday. The caller was a woman. She gave her name as Tabitha Flower, and added what turned out to be Tabitha Flower's correct home address. No, he couldn't remember anything special about her voice. It had been and continued to be a very busy day. Just a voice. Just a woman.

Was the ad to be repeated, and if so, how often? No, just a one-time, said McPharrie. When the check for the ad arrived, would he follow up and see that it was photocopied and have the copy sent to Anne Pence at the following address?

In Cowan's office, Blaine said, "I don't think we ought to make a big dustup about it, blow it out of all proportion, send out a barrage of press releases."

"I agree," Cowan said calmly.

"Have Anne route any and all calls from the press to my office. *If* there are any press calls. It's so damned obviously malice, or some crazyhead at play."

If malice, whose malice? was Cowan's mental question to himself. His first thought, when he was told about the woman caller, was Candide North. Dictating, over the telephone, an ad Walker had written. No, it didn't seem Walker's style, this small-print kick in the groin; or at least what he knew of the outer Walker. Doing it on her own, perhaps. Hell in this case having no fury like the woman whose husband has been scorned.

He tried to summon up what he could of her, from Belding's annual executive party aboard Kellyng's yacht. She was hard to bring clearly to mind: a small, quiet, sun-browned woman whose appearance suggested pottering about the garden and feeding her birds and goldfish. But, quiet waters run deep. Quiet people can harbor dangerous fires under their unrippled surfaces.

Anyone with half a brain could cover herself by using Kellyng's secretary's name and address. Unless Tabitha Flower herself had gone around some menopausal bend and thought it would be fun to begin tottering the empire? A ridiculous idea.

He shouldn't be giving it this much attention. An isolated incident. It wouldn't, though, would it, be the beginning of something? Success can attract hatred, even deranged hatred, like a magnet. The greater the success, the more powerful the pull of the magnet.

The Group's eight companies employed about thirteen thousand people. Any one of them—

But why should it be a Belding employee?

It could be anyone, anyone in the world.

Yes, an isolated incident. Swat the mosquito. Don't notice that it has left the tiniest flick of blood to stain the sleeve of your immaculate shirt.

CHAPTER 7

Ada Kellyng sat at breakfast on Tuesday in the dining room of the main house of the Kellyng compound at Palm Springs. She was alone because her husband was sleeping late, a practice of which she disapproved. "Better for the circulation to be up and about, Herbert," she invariably chided when at last, at about eleven, he was up and about.

There were a great many things of which Ada Kellyng disapproved. She had channeled her disapproval into action and last year had founded her Moral Quorum, which in one way or another had gained national notice. It fought its idea of vice and general backsliding across the board: in television programs and commercials, in movies, popular records, clothing, publishing. Its composition was about three-quarters women and one-quarter men. The female voice, mainly, could be heard uplifted in wrath, from New York to San Francisco, addressing meetings the size of which grew steadily.

"It's a nice little hobby of hers," Kellyng would explain to the lifted eyebrows of his colleagues. She was not, as he was, amiably Quaker; but bedrock Scots Presbyterian. The Quorum didn't, he felt no necessity to add, hurt the Belding Group in the subtly changing moral climate of the country.

She had gone to a meeting in Dallas on Monday and was catching up, over her own orchard-grown grapefruit and sugarless tea, with yesterday's mail. Gratifying, the thick bundle of what she supposed might be called fan letters.

In an envelope of not very good quality, a black-and-white

snapshot was enclosed within the folded plain white sheet of paper. Mrs. Kellyng looked at the snapshot, uttered a cry like a startled parakeet, put it down, and turned her attention to the letter.

"Dear Mrs. Kellyng, There was a yard sale down our street and I bought a pretty hand-painted box. It turned out to be full of a jumble of old photos. Believe me I was shocked to come on this one. Unless he's got a twin, this looks like the man who has just been elected president of an organization that I heard somewhere your husband has something to do with. I thought you ought to see it. What are we coming to? I had a great-uncle, a bank vice-president, and he was never seen out of a full suit of clothes, he did not believe even in shirtsleeves in the worst hot weather. I plan to boycott all Belding Co. products and have advised my friends to do so too. Yours sincerely (signature all but unreadable), Brooklyn, N. Y.

Mrs. Kellyng forced herself to look at the photograph again. After all, most people were supposed to have doubles. Her close gaze stopped at the base of the man's throat.

The camera's subject was a man standing, nude and powerful, on a jutting rock, glinting water behind him, an equally naked and slender young woman apparently sunning herself, lying flat on a towel on the rock.

The *face* looked like Cowan, a younger Cowan, but the all-but-unmistakable eyebrows and cheekbones. With shrinking fingers she turned the mat-finished oblong of paper over and saw scrawled on the back, "Mal and Jessie, Sorrento." No year given.

Mal. Malcolm. A relatively uncommon name. Malcolm Cowan.

Acting on instinct—was it because in some frightful way she couldn't erase the picture from her mind, not one detail of the picture?—she tore it across and across again. There was an ashtray at Herbert's place across from her. He liked a pipe after breakfast, however scolded by his wife. "It's my one pipe of the day, dear."

She put the pieces in the ashtray, picked up the sterling silver pipe lighter, and set them afire. She watched until they were blackened, let them cool, and then shook the ashtray into a leather wastebasket. She found herself trembling all over, and in a fury that in someone else she would have called self-indulgent and non-constructive.

When Kellyng came downstairs to what he had expected to be a peaceful plate of bacon and eggs, he got from his wife the full blast of the communication from Brooklyn. He read the letter, pausing with a lengthened face at the word "boycott." "But where," he asked, "is this picture of Cowan, *maybe* Cowan?"

"It was absolutely disgusting. I burned it. Not a stitch on. Beside a lake. A girl without a stitch on, either, lounging about at his feet."

"Gracious," said Kellyng.

"You'll have to speak to him. Maybe he does this kind of thing every summer weekend."

"Hardly, in a condominium. He and Agatha have just bought one."

"Well, before that didn't they have a place in Marin County as well as the house in San Francisco?" Erax was based in San Francisco; Cowan had lived there for the seven years between his divorce and his move to the Belding presidency, and to New York. "Of course there would have been a swimming pool. The Lord knows what goings-on . . ."

"I suppose for both our sakes," said fair-minded Kellyng, "Belding's, that is, and his own, he deserves notification."

Kellyng had not yet been informed of the want ad in the *Times*; the less he knew about it, Miss Flower had decided, the better. Considering his heart condition.

Cowan had just returned from a meeting with Nocella

Foods, where the matter under consideration was whether this giant of packaged dry and frozen Italian foods should pick up a small but increasingly successful competitor, Maggiore. The line was upper-price and generally sold through gourmet shops or departments, but in the peculiar pattern of American purchasing, so-called luxury items were vanishing from the shelves like giveaways. Just as expensive cars, and expensive clothes, and expensive housing, were selling as though there were no such thing as money troubles in the country.

After listening to all the facts presented, Cowan made use of one of his well-known pauses. His silences were as dramatic as his soft, sure voice. He looked at his strong hands, palms down, fingers spread, on the burled mahogany surface of the conference table. One could almost hear the hum of his brain.

Then, "My suggestion is, buy it," he said. After a glance at his watch, "And good afternoon to you, gentlemen."

Anthony Nocella caught up with him as he was leaving the room. "Too bad," he said darkly, "about Walker North."

"Yes. Too bad." He offered no explanations, no smoothing over, but with his demanding brilliant stare left Nocella in the position where he himself must offer them.

"I suppose that under the circumstances he thought he couldn't—I mean—well, he's got nothing to worry about, he ought to be picked up in no time flat. I understand some Russian drug firm approached him a few months back, wanting him to Americanize their whole distribution and marketing scene."

"Ah," said Cowan.

In his office, he took the call from Kellyng, who first wished him good-day and then without preamble asked lightly, "Are you given to bathing in the nude in mixed company, Mal? What they, I'm told, call skinny-dipping."

"No," said Cowan. "Why?"

"Well, someone sent my wife—who as you may know

heads up a little morals group—a picture that purports to be of you." He censored slightly his wife's description of the photograph. And didn't add that the location was Sorrento because Mrs. Kellyng in her outrage had forgotten this small and to her unimportant detail. It was being naked that mattered, not *where* you were naked.

"I'll send along the letter, which threatens a sales boycott. Tempest in a teapot, probably. But it does remind us," voice still gentle, "that we never know, do we, who's looking over our back fence."

After farewell pleasantries were exchanged, Cowan sat very still at his desk. He felt a rare sensation, an interior trembling of confused rage.

No matter how nicely put, a reprimand had just been handed to him.

He had been scolded, in essence. By the chairman.

Think back. Maybe several times, years ago, on vacations abroad, or at a private house or so on Long Island, among gaily partying people who thought nothing about stripping to the skin . . .

"*She burned it.*" He saw himself in Mrs. Kellyng's appalled eyes. Unclothed and therefore unclean. And there was no way now to prove her wrong, if the picture was of some other man.

Oh well, Christ, just another mosquito to swat. Like last Friday's. He supposed he could expect more of the same. Just get your name and your picture—and your new eminence—in the newspapers and out they came crawling, the hidden haters, from under their rocks.

Early in the afternoon of the previous Thursday, Nick undertook a project Jane had suggested several days before. "When you get to it, no great hurry": cleaning out the attic of the brownstone. He said to Jane, "If you'll come up with me for a few minutes and just put a little chalk mark on anything you want to keep, it would be a great help."

The possessions-owning part of Jane was, in spite of deep and recent shock, still functioning in its separate compartment. They took the elevator to the fourth floor, climbed the steep attic stairs, and she began rapidly chalking. On a cobwebbed shelf, she saw the wooden box, painted with zinnias and yellow butterflies, in which she had been in the habit of tossing, long ago, photographs which for one reason or another she wanted to save.

"I forgot about this pretty box," she said aloud, either to herself or to Nick. "I think I'll take it down with me and clear it out. I can use it on the desk in the sitting room."

CHAPTER 8

At five o'clock on Tuesday Dana flipped the cover over her typewriter. She picked up the Spode cup and saucer she had borrowed from the butler's pantry for afternoon tea, and went to the kitchen to wash and return the flowery china to its shelf.

It was a large room, the kitchen, blue-and-white fresh, its two windows overlooking the back garden. An attractive place at all times and more so now with Nick Quinn busily at work in it.

"Just in time," he said. "Have some caviar, Dana."

She lifted the linen napkin over a sterling silver plate, helped herself to a finger of hot buttered toast, spread it with the caviar, squeezed lemon over it, and added grated egg yolk. She ate this with joyful greed as she watched him mixing martinis in a little crystal pitcher.

Why was everything heightened, the flavor of the caviar, the late evening sun in the ginkgo tree branches moving against one of the windows, when he was a few feet away?

"Who's the caviar for?"

"Vice-president of Manufacturers Hanover Trust to cocktails upstairs."

He saw her looking with mild amusement at the businesslike white apron over his chinos. "The sauce spatters," he explained, gesturing at the stove.

"I wondered what smelled so marvelous. What is it?"

He moved to her, put one arm around her, and in a leisurely and experimental way kissed her mouth.

"Spaghetti sauce."

"What's in it?"

"Oregano, basil, parsley, onions, garlic, fresh lemon juice, and, oh yes, tomatoes. You're all pink, Dana."

"Do you usually go around kissing everybody in sight?"

"No. Only a select few."

Without being aware of it she put a finger to her lips, lips now with a startling discovery to add to their memories.

"The backstairs help rollicking and romping in the kitchen," she said lightly, as if to dismiss to herself something that for a flash had seemed important out of all proportion. "By that I mean both of us, of course. I mean, the word 'help' applies to both of us."

"Rollicking? Romping? A friendly kiss is not exactly my idea of getting down to it, behind the scenes. But have it your own way."

He went and got two crystal cocktail glasses from the butler's pantry. "Wait here, will you, while I take this stuff upstairs. There's something I want to talk to you about."

Another little romp? A move closer to really getting down to it?

He smiled as though reading her mind and said, "The word was *talk*, Dana. Actually you're safe as houses with me."

Actually, that, a little while back, was nothing. Actually, aren't you taking yourself a bit seriously, my poor girl?

She waited for him uncertainly, a little off balance.

When he came back he said, "You look like a trustworthy soul. If I tell you something, will you promise to keep it to yourself? Because for some reason I can't keep it to *myself*."

She nodded, and he went on, "Last Thursday night when I was emptying the office wastebaskets I came on something a little odd. In Jane's basket. Her gold pencil was sitting at the bottom of it, must have rolled off the edge of the desk. I fielded the pencil and right underneath I saw a piece of paper with her handwriting on it . . ."

Listening—eavesdropping—was a shameful thing.

Midge, who had just been coming into the butler's pantry from the hall, wanting from the kitchen refrigerator a drink of cold orange juice, stopped six inches over the threshold. The pantry was at right angles to the open door into the kitchen and from where she stood she could not be seen by the two inside.

". . . with her handwriting on it, the words jumping right up at me, 'Excellent opportunity for right person.' Jane Frame, Inc. as far as I know doesn't place ads for executive personnel in newspapers, and if anyone had to go to the trouble to write one, it would be Midge. Do you agree?"

"Yes," Dana said, her curiosity at a high flare.

"Well, I read the ad, thinking she might have an idea of replacing me. And I happen to like it here. Everything"—he gazed thoughtfully into her violet eyes—"about it, stem to stern. It was the ad that ran in the *Times* Friday, wanting a new president for Belding. Now, Dana, clear this up for me. Tell me why. Why would Jane either stoop to such a thing or rise to such dizzy heights of fantasy, depending on how you look at it?"

"I have no idea," Dana said slowly. "It's a little . . . scary, isn't it?" The thought of the brilliantly practical, the all-but-humorless Jane up to explosive fun and games in print rang impossibly false.

And in spite of that, on the evidence, was the plain unanswerable truth.

Nick was coming down the carpeted marble stairs to the entrance hall, having delivered a second helping of martinis, when he heard the sound of a key in the lock of the front door. It opened and Walker North strode in.

He hadn't known until now that North had his own key to the house. He did know that North was warmly welcome here, bodily involved with Jane, unless they carried on absorbed conversations about pharmaceuticals late into the night and often until the following morning.

Although a bit puzzled about Jane's classy houseman, Walker had firmly placed him as the Help, and in a suitable tone of voice said, "Good evening, Quinn. Is Miss Frame at home?"

"Yes, in her sitting room, entertaining a banker."

"Is he to stay on for dinner?"

"No. Dinner for two ordered, Miss Frame and Miss Teller. It's Miss Teller's birthday."

"Then I'll go up and wait."

The second floor held, as well as Jane's comfortable firelit sitting room, the library and her large bedroom and bath. Nick wondered idly which room North would choose to wait in. Sandwiched between the banker and Midge's spaghetti feast, there seemed little time for amorous dalliance.

Jane saw her guest to the door and went back upstairs to change from her chalk-striped Bill Blass suit into an at-home dress. Her bedroom had an occupant, sitting sideways on the long graceful chair by the window which Jane never used; she was not a lounger.

"*Walker.*" She felt an absurd rush of joy and relief; absurd because she shouldn't have allowed the shadow of a doubt that he would ever be back.

He rose, and very deliberately as she approached him slipped his hands into his pockets. There was to be no embrace, then.

Or, not until she had rearranged the scene as she wished it to be played. She might need a little time for that.

"Stay still, I have to go downstairs for a moment."

Midge wouldn't mind having her birthday dinner postponed, obliging accommodating Midge.

Her office door was closed. There was a note taped to it.

"Dear Jane, I'm leaving now (5:20) to go straight home. Appointments all cleaned up. I'm terribly sorry about dinner, may we have it another night? I've felt ill all afternoon, nothing serious but I'd be better off with a cup of tea and bed. Midge."

Good. Although one hoped it was indeed nothing serious; Midge was never, never out sick.

Returning to Walker, who was still standing with his hands in his pockets, by the window, she said, "You've been very much in my mind since Thursday, as you can well imagine. I must say you look marvelous."

"I thought I'd get away for a bit—from the phone calls from kind friends and the paragraph or so in *The Wall Street Journal* and maybe the *Times*. Candide and I went up to my brother's hunting place in the Adirondacks. Believe it or not, I caught some trout." Voice casual; detached. Blade-nosed face fresh with sun and air, exercise and rest.

Was this to be his only reference to his firing? Was her help and sympathy and strength to be thrust aside?

"Walker, what happened?"

"You know what happened."

"But why and how?"

"He had it all set up. He used his electric goad on me. I said a few natural hasty things, and he said that it was a bore and counterproductive to have hurt feelings around, and that we'd call it a parting by mutual agreement." Now, in addition to the fresh color, there were sharp red patches on his cheekbones.

She wanted to move closer to him, put her arms around him, but for the moment couldn't climb over the invisible wall between them.

Naturally, under that calm, he's hurt to the bone, Jane thought, wanting to strike out at everything and everybody. Even at me.

Patience was indicated, something she had very little of.

"That's behind us," she said firmly. "I've had several ideas—"

He cut across her. "I have prospects of my own that may shape up, but I don't want to think of them just now. Amazing how pleasant—briefly—freedom is. Candide's ambassadorial uncle bought a little place for his retirement in Paris, on Île St. Louis, and we're going to take a couple of weeks there. Leaving tomorrow, so that . . ." Now he came over to her and lightly took her hand. "Until another time, Jane."

One part of her mind said, It's simply bravura, and not unwise of him at that. Showing all the world that instead of presenting a picture of rejection and distress, Walker North was disporting himself in Paris, and having a lovely time, thank you.

The other part said, This can't be happening, his waiting for you in your bedroom, and then leaving you cold there. Very cold. A bedroom scene without a bedroom plot.

He dropped her hand, went to the door, and closed it quietly behind him.

Midge made more than enough money to be transported about New York by taxi, but she was of an economical bent and any extravagance on her part—for herself, not for others—made her feel vaguely guilty.

Midge by name and Midge by nature, she had often told herself in mild rebellion. When she had joined Jane's agency, she had said, "I think this might be the right time to go back to Mildred. I'd like to. It sounds, I don't know, more whole."

"No," Jane said. "Midge makes a nice easy-going counterpoint to the, admit it, forthright syllables, Jane Frame."

"Oh, all right," said Midge.

Outrage was a feeling rare to her, but she was possessed by outrage in the Fifth Avenue bus on her way downtown and home. It was in response to the deepest emotion and strongest loyalty she had ever felt for anyone in her entire life.

He had once, at a Christmas party at Pursloe, kissed her, not a fumbling drunken kiss but a direct and powerful caress. "You are not only the world's best Girl Friday, Midge, but Mondays, Tuesdays, Wednesdays, and Thursdays too. Thank you for taking such good care of me. Merry, merry Christmas."

Her apartment was on West Ninth Street between Fifth and Sixth, on the second floor of a white-painted brick house which pleasantly interrupted the brownstone fronts. She had lived there for fifteen years. A pet of her landlord because she was so quiet there, so prompt with her rent, so undemanding in matters of painting and repairs, she paid less than the going rate of this pretty street.

She had made it up, about being ill, in the note to Jane on her door. She could not for anything on earth sit down tonight at a candlelit table with Jane, only Jane, across from her. And eat her favorite dinner of roast beef and spaghetti. And open up the parcel by her plate, which would have something frightfully expensive in it. Now, going up her stairs, she did feel a little ill and a little dizzy.

Excellent opportunity for right person. The malice of it. The desire to injure, like a bad child hurling a stone.

Was Jane planning to hurl other stones?

She well knew that Jane harbored a cold dislike for Malcolm Cowan. Not entirely unnatural, Midge had thought in her way of always trying to understand. What sifted out of the gossip at the time of the divorce was that he had left Jane, not the other way around; that he had initiated the whole thing. Well, she, Midge, knew what it felt like to be walked out upon. Or had for a short time. The dominating image of Cowan had long since wiped out any picture of her husband, Leonard, from her mind, or any emotion whatever about him.

In her bedroom, she undressed to her slip and put on a bathrobe. She thought about tea and decided a little whiskey would be a better idea, steadying. It might also supply her with the needed courage.

For what? For this.

Don't do it by hand, he might even after all these years recognize and remember her handwriting. She turned to the portable typewriter on its table at right angles to her desk. Get it down roughly. Then smooth and retype it.

"Dear Mr. Cowan, I think that you should be informed that it was Jane Frame who wrote and placed the ad concerning a new president for the Belding Group in last Friday's *Times*."

She wouldn't sign her name, of course, just, "A well-wisher" —or something like that.

Her heart was pounding heavily. He'd read it and if she knew Malcolm Cowan he'd go directly to Jane and face her with it.

What if the omniscient Jane found out who had written him with this information?

What if, in her sometimes terrifying way of diving for and finding essentials, she began the relentlessly accurate thought chain: Who could have known this and written him? Was I stupid enough—or angry enough, beside myself—to have left the penciled draft in my wastebasket? Who, then, would have access to it? Nick Quinn. Dana. And Midge.

At my age, Midge thought, foreseeing with clarity the thunderstorm bursting over her head, where would I find a job as good, or a decent job at all, with attractive people in their twenties and thirties elbowing their elders aside? And probably with a blackball from Jane: Don't hire the Teller woman, she's absolutely not to be trusted and as you know this is a field where discretion is a must.

You coward.

A man can fight back and take care of himself if he knows who's after him.

But when he doesn't know, he can be reduced after a time

to a state of quivering helplessness. Even a man like Malcolm Cowan.

She rolled a sheet of anonymous white bond paper into the typewriter, put down the date, and copied the message she had composed. Including the typed sign-off, "A well-wisher."

She should go out and post it right away, before she lost her courage and tore it up and—with a glance at her own wastebasket—flushed it down the toilet.

But a great fatigue descended, making her feel boneless, incapable of motion, in her little swivel chair.

CHAPTER 9

"Just the important things, Anne, I'm in a hurry," Cowan said at five-thirty on Friday when Anne came in with the interoffice and delivered mail.

He had arrived back from France this morning. His task there, successfully accomplished, had been to throw his weight into negotiations for borrowing a large sum of money from the Banque de France to finance a new Redoubté facility in Marseilles.

Conferences had kept him busy all day, and tonight he was to be guest speaker at the annual dinner of the Society of Economists. He was, even for his notable staying powers, tired.

She placed various papers in front of him for his signature, adding a brief explanation where necessary. "That's all for now, the rest will keep till Monday. Oh—here's this."

A long plain white envelope, with PERSONAL AND CONFIDENTIAL typed in the lower left-hand corner. He looked at it without interest, obviously thinking of something else. "My attaché case is somewhere in the lounge. Will you find it and transcribe the tapes of the Redoubté meetings, please. I'll want them first thing Monday."

The lounge was the Belding name for the great window-walled living room which formed part of his office quarters. Anne always felt vicariously wealthy when she had occasion to enter it.

Cowan slit open the white envelope and took out the

folded sheet of paper. The note took approximately three and one-half seconds to read but the time seemed much longer than that. Time had in a way suspended itself.

Anne, looking at him through the glass dividing wall, was a little puzzled at his posture. He was sitting at his desk with his elbows out at right angles to his torso, shoulders raised, palms flat, grasping the desk edge, his head inclined over the sheet of paper on the desk. He was seldom as motionless as this for long.

His appearance, it occurred to her, was that of a man bracing himself to charge something or someone unseen. She found this, if fascinating, a bit frightening too.

I wouldn't, Anne thought, like to be in the path of this particular catapult.

For some reason not wanting him to catch her eye, to know he was being visually eavesdropped on at this strange moment —or was it minutes?—she turned her back. She continued, facing the other direction toward the end wall of the room, to collect from his case the Redoubté meeting tapes.

But—suppose he was ill, trying to cope with a sudden emergency of the heart? She had nothing to go on as she had only worked for him for two weeks. His secretary at Erax hadn't wanted to leave San Francisco and move East, not even for her beloved Mr. Cowan. Anne had occupied her present post under Cyrus Fane, who had been president of the Belding Group until at fifty-nine he was forced into retirement by the board.

She stole a glance over her shoulder. Thank heavens he was moving, or at least one of his hands was. The hand crumpled the sheet of paper into a ball. Then, opening his palm, he looked at the crumple, smoothed it out, folded it, and put it in his billfold.

He got up from his desk and without so much as a good-evening glance in her direction left his office.

His speech before five hundred people in a banqueting room at the Waldorf, on "An Economic Forecast of the Eighties" drew a great deal of applause, perhaps not so much because of its content, which was safe-and-sound, but because of the speaker himself. He was eye-bolting in his black dinner jacket, addressing his audience with the magnetic quietness of an authority that knew it never had to raise its voice to hold attention.

After the speech, he allowed himself to be lionized for a time, personally introduced here and there, while flash bulbs blued the candlelit prosperous scene.

A heavy hand clapped him on the shoulder. It belonged to Dan Wyler, president of the nationwide fast-food chain, Pit Burgers, a Belding Group member. "Let's get out of this mess and have a quiet chat in a corner," Wyler said. "I'll scurry up a couple of drinks for us." Cowan knew that the other man wished to suggest to onlookers his close companionship, his right to intimacy, with the new Belding president; however, weary, he agreed.

In a corner secluded behind a pillar, Wyler first offered, "great stuff, your speech." He was a man who prided himself on his brashness ("Never screw around, go straight to the point, that's my motto"). "Now then—what's the inside dope on Walker North?"

"Inside dope?" Cowan enunciated the words as though they were in some foreign language he didn't understand. "It was a matter of, simply, mutual agreement. He had hoped for the job, and I got it."

"Hell, I'm mining a dry well," Wyler said. "I thought it might be something really hairy—that he'd come at you with a dagger or something. And, I heard that he might have been thinking of walking off with Greave."

Cowan finished his drink. "Absolutely without foundation."

"Maybe his Jane will comfort him and find him a job even

bigger than yours, heading up General Motors or DuPont or something."

"Jane? I believe his wife's name is Candide."

"Didn't you know?" Now Wyler was enjoying himself, imparting fresh information to what he had thought were all-hearing ears; even more fun because it concerned Cowan's ex-wife. "He and Jane Frame are, or have been, at it hot and heavy. Could be just gossip but—"

"Ah. I had no idea. But then I don't interest myself in gossip. And now I'll wish you good night, Dan. Nice to see you."

"Drop by for a Pit Burger on the house in any one of fifty states, when you're in the mood," said Wyler.

At ten o'clock on Saturday morning Cowan, in his study in the condominium on Fifth Avenue overlooking Central Park, called Jane.

"Hello?" On Saturdays and Sundays, Jane did not identify herself when answering the telephone.

"Hello, Jane, it's Malcolm."

She had never used to him the shortening of his name to one syllable; she disliked the nickname.

"Is it. I'd forgotten what your voice sounded like."

"Yes, it is. Surname, Cowan. I called to invite you out to dinner tonight."

"Why?"

Because I am going to see you face to face, and if I were to ring the bell and walk into your house you are perfectly capable of calling the police to have me ejected.

"Why? Last I heard you were in business—quite successfully so—and I have several things to discuss with you."

"Sorry, dinner party tonight. Here."

"Lunch, then."

"When? Today?"

"Yes, today."

"All right, where?"

"Leo's. One o'clock."

Jane's voice throughout the brief conversation had been flat and cool, without the lift and fall of any kind of surprise or any emotion whatever.

Now she expelled a long breath as she replaced the receiver. An intense excitement began to rise in her.

Under no circumstances could she imagine Malcolm Cowan busying himself in the recruitment of personnel for Belding.

Under no circumstances could she have brought herself to refuse the lunch invitation.

There is no point, she told herself, in stamping on someone's foot unless you can hear the howl of pain. Sooner or later.

He was strong and he was brainy; but she felt that in both departments she outstripped him.

She might be one of many to whom the gauntlet was being thrown down. After the little land mine in the *Times*, after the photograph dispatched to Mrs. Kellyng of the Moral Quorum, he would of course be wondering which of many people who had reason to dislike or hate him would have been responsible for these perpetrations.

In a possible campaign on his part of personally interviewing everyone on his enemies' list, she wondered where she stood. It was tempting to think she was at or near the top of the list.

But the lovely thing was, he wouldn't, now or ever, be able to prove anything. He'd have to try to frighten somebody into ceasing and desisting. She didn't frighten easily; as of right now, she didn't frighten at all.

Wait a minute. Could it be (disappointingly) something about Walker North? He might easily have heard about their affair. She had never troubled herself with concealment because as always it was her practice to take openly whatever she wanted. The usual rules, the discretion, secrecy, were for other people.

Could he have had second thoughts about firing Walker and want, through this special intermediary, to renegotiate the firing? Sorry, Malcolm, he's in Paris with Candide having the time of his life.

Leo's was the current insider's eating place, drawing custom from La Grenouille, Lutèce, and Laparouse. The walls of the tall rooms were of white-painted trelliswork mounted on mirror, the chairs were lacy white wrought iron, and a fountain in a flower-rimmed pool centered each room.

"Good afternoon, Mr. Cowan." The headwaiter conducted him to a reserved table in the mysteriously best of the three rooms to be seen lunching in. "A drink while you wait?"

Something told him that Jane, measurably prompt to the tick of a second, would be deliberately late. "Yes, scotch, please. Milk and ice on the side." An ulcer from years back was, as it usually did at times of extreme stress, muttering at him.

He had finished the scotch and was sipping the milk when Jane arrived at one-fifteen. She wore a black suit, a severe white silk shirt, and no makeup whatever. As if to say, For this lunch, for you, the plainest of Janes will do.

They had not met face to face for seven years. Jane crisply ordered Perrier water and when the waiter went off said, "The man who does your hair is quite good."

"Thanks." He offered no return back-of-my-hand comment or compliment. "What do you think you're up to, Jane?"

"Up to?" She didn't even blink. The gray eyes met his levelly. He recognized and interpreted accurately the cold silver sparkle of the eyes: she was excited, she was enjoying herself, and behind the large pale forehead the mind was formidably at work.

"The *Times* ad. The photograph, taken at what might be called an informal swimming party."

"Is this a prepared questionnaire to be used at random? I did see the ad. Odd, wasn't it. I know nothing of any photograph."

The waiter, sensing a singular lack of festivity at this table for two, came to inquire about their food orders.

"Entrecôte, rare," said Jane.

"The duck à l'orange," said Cowan.

From nowhere the wine waiter appeared. "Hardly," Jane said to Cowan, "on top of your milk."

"How wifely of you. Bring me a half bottle of Bocuse Rhone."

Her voice was equally cold. "How small-boy defiant of you."

Two tables away, a man said to a woman, "There's the Great Auk."

"Who?"

"Jane Frame, no less. With I *think* her ex-husband. King Cowan. Belding."

"If you're right, it's just as well they're not married anymore. One feels a slight chill even at this safe distance."

"I'm curious," Jane said in an idle fashion. "Why on earth did you associate me with these executive pinpricks?"

He had no intention of informing her about his Friday afternoon mail. The "well-wisher" could very easily be someone in close proximity to her, an associate, a secretary, and punishment might be swiftly meted out. For some reason he had never for a moment doubted the bare-boned truth of the note.

"I'd heard you've been sleeping with Walker North and thought his departure from the Group might have prompted the, in your words, pinpricks. Besides, there's a woman-y feel to them. And with most women I get on quite well."

Except for—hanging in the air between them—the one I shed for good and all, thank Christ.

After that, Cowan made no attempt to break the silence before their food arrived, contenting himself with fastening his eyes on Jane's face in a relentless brilliant stare. She, in turn, stared at his neck above the plum-and-white striped shirt collar, which made him, several times, swallow convulsively in spite of himself.

Picking up his knife and fork, he said, "Don't think any target too easy. I am not a sitting duck, waiting to be shot, retrieved, cleaned, stuffed, roasted, and served with orange."

"Are you saying you will go after some imaginary single adversary and—what?—take him to court?"

"To my own court," Cowan said. "So far, you've just been amusing yourself. No real harm done. But, lay off, Jane." The discreetly lowered soft voice added power to his threat, or warning. "I can hit back and hurt back very hard. To stop you cold."

Jane offered no immediate response to this but ate her entrecôte and endive salad with appetite. Then, touching her mouth corners with her napkin, she raised her clear voice.

"Actually, I could do with something after my life has been threatened." At the next table, a glass of Pouilly Fousse on its way to rosy lips paused in mid-air. "Order me a double brandy, will you."

The deep uncontrollable red of fury swept Cowan's face. He seemed to feel the eyes burning into his skin, dozens of pairs of eyes around the room, and to hear the words repeated over and over in the listening ears.

The bitch. The bloody bitch.

He ordered the brandy and raising his own voice said agreeingly, "Well, in your neighborhood it's wise to be on your guard at all times. You *are* still on Seventy-third Street?"

She disposed of her brandy in three quick swallows. "Yes. Safe and well—and sane—on Seventy-third Street. And now if you won't mind I'll leave you. Our business for today is quite finished, isn't it?"

She got up and walked out of the restaurant.

"My wife told me a strange thing," said Howell of Coastal Petroleum to Devlin of ITT. "She was having lunch at Leo's yesterday. Cowan and Jane Frame—she's his ex, you know—were a few tables away. Frame accused Cowan of making a threat on her life."

CHAPTER 10

Let him think for a little while that now all is well, that I've swallowed and disgested his warning, Jane instructed herself. Then it will come as even more of a shock when—

Very much against his will, and his pride, Cowan instituted security precautions in his immediate personal circle.

On their return from the eleven o'clock service at St. Thomas's Episcopal Church ten blocks down Fifth Avenue from their condominium, he and Agatha settled themselves to their Sunday midday brunch of bloody marys and eggs Benedict.

For some reason briefing his wife was more difficult than dropping a bomb of unpleasant news on an entire board of directors. After a fortifying pull at his drink, Cowan began, "It won't be the first time or the last, Agatha, but at the moment I have a form of hit man on my heels. Only it isn't a man, it's a woman."

Agatha was a tall woman with a strong plain freckled face and sandy-red hair. ("In the way of the French saying that a man always falls in love with the same woman," a friend of Cowan's remarked, "Cowan runs true to form. Plain women with lots of money.") She was very much in love with him and at his announcement her freckles seemed to grow darker as her skin briefly paled.

"Not," he hastened to add, "with a gun. Only vicious heckling, an attempt at public and professional embarrassment. And the only reason I trouble you with it is that she is not under any circumstances to be admitted to this apartment. You never in your social wanderings happened to run across Jane Frame, did you?"

"But she was your—oh." Agatha thought she saw and was reassured. Old jealousies, resentments, nothing really frightening to cope with. "No, I've never met her. Of course one's heard of her. High-powered career type."

"More than that. She's turned into somewhat of a wild bull of a woman and is not easily turned aside from any goal, however mad it may be."

"Can't you get a restraining order or something?"

"No—nothing illegal so far. But, listen carefully, and pass it along to the servants." He gave her a coldly accurate verbal portrait of Jane. "Not that she's likely to turn up here, but in any case so you'd know her if she did."

"Then she was the one who ran that *Times* ad?"

"Yes, and a few other things I won't bore you with."

A possessive rage gripped Agatha. A woman—a *woman*—out to chastise her dauntless Mal. A woman who had once been married to him, who had had her share of him for years.

"Don't worry," she said hotly. "I'll be more than ready if and when I come across her."

"No spats in public, Agatha. That's just what she'd adore, grist to her mill, gossip columns, and so on."

Agatha deliberately calmed her face. She took a sip of her bloody mary. "Certainly not," she agreed hastily, finishing the sentence to herself, "in public."

Anne Pence, on Monday morning, got the same briefing and was quite unruffled about it. So many of these big men, in her experience, had someone in the shadows from whom they cowered. Cyrus Fane had given her keep-off instructions pertaining to a cook his wife had fired, who had sworn to kill Fane at the first opportunity, with a meat ax she had taken from the Fane kitchen upon her abrupt departure.

"Not that she's apt to turn up here," Cowan said again. "But, forewarned."

Agatha went to the kitchen for a short session with Mrs. Kramer, the cook, the daily maid Rita, and the Vietnamese houseman, Tan.

"There's a woman who's been making a nuisance of herself to Mr. Cowan," she told them. "She's not to be let in if she comes here. I will describe her to you."

How awkward, how strange this all sounded, coming from her own lips. The splendid Mr. Cowan barring his twelve-room condominium to one single human being, and a woman at that? She was listened to with breathless interest by the three.

". . . and auburn—well, reddish-brown hair, parted on one side. Her name is Jane Frame," she finished. "If there are any telephone calls from her, of course you will note them down."

In a small attempt at recovering something, confidence or dignity or both, she said, "And, Rita, bring me another pot of coffee, please."

Making the fresh coffee, Mrs. Kramer said to Rita, "Some woman after him. *Well!* You couldn't exactly knock me over with a feather."

"I wonder if he knows she's told us all about this," Rita said. She giggled. "I mean, it sounds like a police description. Five feet eight inches, fair skin, gray eyes, and all that."

"This woman wanted," said Mrs. Kramer, falling into the spirit of the thing, "by Mr. Malcolm Cowan. Oh, my stars."

Agatha, at a slow deep simmer, drank her coffee while she spent a half hour in unaccustomed reading: *The Wall Street Journal* and the business section of the New York *Times*.

She went to her bedroom, closed the door, studied the telephone directory in its apple-green velvet cover, and dialed. "Jane Frame Agency," said a pleasant young voice, female.

"I'm Anthea Rowan. I'd like an appointment with Miss

Frame, the sooner the better. I am a designer of computers. I've been with Tesselman in Zurich, but now I prefer to relocate in this country. I'm afraid I'm in rather a high bracket. I'm in touch with Erax in California and Bookington in Savannah, but I thought while I was in New York . . ."

"Please hold on for just a moment or so. I'll give you something to listen to while you're waiting." The "Rachmaninoff Piano Concerto Number One" began playing into Agatha's startled ear. The music faded gently as the girl's voice said, "Tomorrow morning at ten, if that will suit you."

"Yes, fine."

In Agatha's world, based as it was on five generations of privilege, you did not sit idly by in meek acceptance. You coped. You took problems into your own two hands, faced and outfaced them. You took bulls, even wild bulls, by their horns.

With a tidied mind, and a sense of being in charge again after that brief moment in the kitchen when things seemed to be oddly askew, to be slipping and sliding, she bathed and dressed.

Lunch at Eleanor's, an afternoon of bridge, at which she herself excelled, a quiet dinner alone with Mal because he liked guestless Monday evenings. Tell Mrs. Kramer to poach the fresh salmon Sigismund Lynas had sent to them from Canada, where he was fishing and hunting for several weeks.

Yes, nice to have things planned, arranged, normal again, going the way she wanted them, again.

It was raining heavily on Tuesday. Although Agatha would not stoop to disguising herself she took a certain comfort in the deeply flopping brim of her beige felt hat and the turned-up collar of her crisply tailored belted raincoat. As a compromise—but surely a successful businesswoman did not answer her own doorbell or knocker—she put on a pair of dark glasses.

Her taxi stopped in front of the brownstone on Seventy-third Street at five minutes of ten. And then the strangeness, totally unanticipated, started.

Her husband had lived in this house for eight years. Gone up these amber-gray marble stairs, between these wrought-iron railings. Opened the door with his own key, how many thousands of times?

She rang, feeling hazed and uncertain and unlike herself. A young woman admitted her but Agatha hardly registered the delightful face and hair. She was in the main entrance hall now, sensing his presence, hearing his footsteps echo on the marble floor and then hush themselves as he started up the long carpeted stairway. To their bedroom. Coming home in the evening, to his wife. If his schedule had been then, as it was now, apt to keep him out often in the evenings, often late, he would, yes, go straight up. He would have had his dinner.

Dana was a little puzzled at the woman's stillness as she stood as though listening to something, or for something. But then the brainy were often a trifle odd, not feeling condemned by any need to please, to conform, to produce the right words at the right time.

"You're Anthea Rowan?" she asked.

"Yes . . ." Almost a sigh, which didn't go with the tailored raincoat and the forthright felt hat.

"If you'd like to take off your coat, it looks rather wet—"

"No, no, I'll keep it on for the moment, thanks." Protection, the coat. She and Mal had bought it at Jaeger's on Regent Street on their last trip to London. On a sunny midday when, after a leisurely stroll, they had had that lovely lunch at the Mirabelle on Curzon Street. Their first journey away together in two years.

"Miss Frame will see you immediately."

Trying to summon her confidence back, Agatha said coolly, "Well, of course. You did say ten o'clock."

She walked with Dana across the reception room and watched the slender hand drop to the doorknob after the light knock. She wanted suddenly to turn and run, run to the door and down the steps and into the street and away.

Her first view of Jane Frame was from the back, a dark tall silhouette standing by one of the long windows against a background of driving rain. Then the woman moved quickly into the warmth and light of the big room. She put out a hand. "I'm Jane Frame. Good morning. Miss? Mrs.? Ms.? Rowan?"

"Mrs. Rowan," through stiff lips.

"Won't you take off your coat and hat, and relax and get warm?" Jane gestured at the merrily hissing fire. Two ruby brocade chairs were set at angles before it. A low table between them held a blue-and-white Meissen coffee service.

But I'm not Mrs. Rowan, Agatha reminded herself. I stopped being Mrs. Rowan when I came into this room. To do—what? This had been his wife, his *wife*, this woman looking so intently at her. Those hands, that mouth, that tall strong body . . .

She felt hampered by the dark glasses, unable to see with total clarity, see what to do and how to do it. She took them off and put them in her pocket.

"Mmmm," Jane said thoughtfully. "Of course. Anthea Rowan. Agatha Cowan. I've seen your pictures taken at horse shows and such things. Odd how people do cling to their rhythms when for some reason or other they choose to offer false names. Some kind of retention of identity, I suppose. You can't really want a job?"

"No." The rehearsed words were somewhere at the back of her emptily ringing mind. Drag them forward.

What had once been the powder room was now a rather grand bathroom for Jane and the occasional client in need. It had two doors, one opening from the entrance hall near the foot of the stairway and the other into Jane's office.

Yesterday, Jane had said, "I'm a bit tired of that Wedgwood blue, Nick. Aubergine, I think. When you find a moment." She felt no need to explain to her houseman that aubergine was French for eggplant; of course he would know.

He had begun his task of painting the walls and ceiling at a quarter of ten. As he was not a man given to whistling at his work, there was nothing to indicate his presence in the bathroom except the sound of the paintbrush, a light skillful slap and swish.

Jane and her client's voice reached him clearly from beyond the door at the office end of the bathroom. He paused for a moment at the change in Jane's voice from easy politeness to drill-in personal.

He felt no impulse to remove himself discreetly. This sounded to him like some kind of curtain going up. Two women on stage. Facing each other.

"You are to stop amusing yourself at my husband's expense. Immediately."

"Amusing myself?" Jane leaned over, resting her elbows on the back of the wing chair, hands cupping her quizzical, composed face.

"You are to leave him, from this moment, strictly alone. Or I will take steps to have your agency blackballed. Not only through Belding, but through other connections. Of which I have a great many."

"Yes," Jane agreed. "Chase Manhattan, IBM, and is it DuPont or Conoco?" She threw back her head and laughed. "Leave *him* alone! My dear." Pity and contempt in the last two words. "Didn't you know? But then, I often didn't, either, when I was in your place."

Agatha refused to walk into the snapping steel trap which would be sprung by the words from her, "Know what?" She stood erect and silent, hands at her sides. A drop of rain fell from the hem of her coat to the shimmer of the Kashan silk rug.

As if in belated kindness, Jane asked gently, "Are you happy with him? I was, for longer than you two have been married, until . . ."

"You are rather a dreadful woman."

"And then early in the year he came full circle. Back to me. Can you imagine—I" She waved a hand at a mass of yellow roses on a corner table. "Those, by the roomful. And the calls, and the notes, and the—just when it's most inconvenient—'Can you meet me in front of the Custom House at six-thirty? There's a new little restaurant, Greek, where we'll be Greek to *them*.' I think I'm getting too old for intrigue, for slipping around corners in the dusk. But to be perfectly frank with you, I feel the second-go-round, for me, is just about finished. Awful to come to the time when you say to yourself your lover is a nuisance. But no doubt you've been in the same boat."

She had nothing personal against Agatha Cowan. The woman, appearing here, was merely a stroke of luck to be seized upon without hesitation. A weapon of another kind to be loaded and fired at Cowan.

Solicitous, she said, "Will you have some hot coffee? Perhaps with a little brandy in it? You look a bit undone."

"I do not believe a word you have said." Agatha felt her hands clenching at her sides. She wanted to hurl herself at the other woman.

"Well, naturally not. That's the way we all survive. It didn't happen. It isn't true. Look the other way. And sometimes it really works, thank God. I'm sorry about this, but when you ordered me to leave him alone, and threatened to attack my professional reputation, you did hit rather a tender spot."

Turning to open the door and leave this place, this woman,

this voice, Agatha's final recollection was of the faint, almost sympathetic smile on Jane Frame's face.

Midge as a rule kept her door part way open when she wasn't interviewing. She liked the glow of the reception room, the sight of Dana, liked being in touch with the comings and goings.

She had another reason for having it open, this morning. So as not to be taken by surprise by Jane, a Jane with a bolt of lightning in her fist.

Yesterday had been a day of pure terror. She had been tempted to stay away, stay home ("I still have this nausea, and a bad headache") but would that look, betrayingly, like hiding? It had been a minute-to-minute busy day for Jane. There had been no faintest flicker of lightning.

She had no way of knowing whether Cowan had acted upon her note, or with a shrug thrown it away; or if it still lay unopened until he returned from somewhere or other on Belding business. It was an awful feeling, not knowing anything. Like having stepped, or been pushed, into an open elevator shaft, and hanging in the air, waiting for gravity to take over and dictate the dark downward plunge.

She saw the raincoated woman crossing the reception room on the way to the door. She had been invited five years ago to Cowan's wedding to Agatha Brinton and recognition flashed. But the near-crouching near-run of this woman bore no resemblance to the remembered posture of Cowan's second wife.

What, in God's name, had Jane done to Cowan's second wife?

"Where to?" the taxi driver asked of the woman who had hailed him and now sat silently in back.

Where to? Plans. Did she have a lunch engagement? If she did, it was far too early anyway. The fitting of three new evening dresses at Bergdorf's—was it scheduled for eleven this morning, or Wednesday? Go home and find out what today was all about.

She gave the driver the address. The familiar numbers were in a way reassuring. Home. Where she lived with Mal, Malcolm Cowan, her husband.

Perhaps call him when she got there? No, she never called him at his office, that was what suburban wives did.

And anyway—how was it she had forgotten?—he wouldn't be there. He had left this morning for a series of conferences with Belding Group member Gruening Breweries, winding up with a speech tomorrow night at the dinner following the annual stockholders' meeting.

And what after all was there to call him about? A woman spitting lies in her face about him, and she stupid enough, disloyal enough, to have been for a moment taken in by them, by the lies, the slander.

Would it not be a clever thing—for some other man, not Mal—to name as an enemy he was avoiding the woman with whom he was having an affair? In case any unkind gossip reached his wife's ears?

Nonsense.

Hanging against the rain, a visual echo of Jane Frame's face smiled at her. In, almost, sympathy.

CHAPTER 11

The exchange in Jane's office had fascinated its hearer in the bathroom; but underneath the fascination was a sense of shock, of scald.

To run your armored tank, all guns firing, into the center of a marriage, for all he knew a happy marriage. To do it with such precise and deadly skill. And to make it up, he was entirely sure, out of the whole cloth.

Not a love affair, between those two. On her part at least, a hate affair.

With a sudden tingle of the fingertips, he realized that at any second or split second she could choose to enter her bathroom. Moving at speed, he pressed the cover back on the paintpot, laid the brush on it, went out in the hall, and closed the door soundlessly behind him. Putting his head into the reception room, he muttered mysteriously, "You think I'm at work in the attic and that I've been up there a good hour." The elevator had a special, hearable clank and whine; he chose the stairs, at a run, the carpet keeping his ascent a secret.

He was halfway up the second flight when Jane did enter her bathroom. She was a good deal better at giving orders than taking them, but her periodontist demanded that she rinse her mouth with warm water and salt seven times daily, and she was due for her third rinse. In the matter of the health of her gums, she bowed to the higher authority.

Just inside the door she paused, eyes scanning the one nearly finished aubergine wall, the tarpaulin neat and snug covering the Connemara marble floor, the closed paintpot sitting on yesterday's New York *Times*. The paint was acrylic-based, she noted, very little smell to it to indicate how recently it had been applied. She put a fingertip to the wall. No, not dry yet.

She did her salt rinse and then went into the reception room. "Dana, where is Nick?"

"In the attic, I think, or I thought I heard him saying something about that an hour or so ago."

"Please go and find him. I want him."

That's strange, so do I, Dana thought. Only, in a quite different sense. It had never, this feeling, declared itself with such crystalline strength until just now.

She took the elevator to the fourth floor and climbed the final, uncarpeted flight. The door at the top was open. One dangling bare electric light bulb provided illumination on this dark rainy morning. There was a scraping sound from a far corner of the cavernous space, behind a great ugly carved Jacobean secretary.

"Nick?"

He appeared from his corner, a putty knife in his hand. "Pane loose," he explained. He stopped and looked at her, where she stood almost directly under the light bulb, her hair a tossed blaze and her eyes deep in shadow.

They walked, very slowly and in an unaware fashion, toward each other. She felt deep in his approaching gaze, lost in it, and then she didn't see his eyes anymore as with slow inevitability his mouth took over.

Or had she started it, lifted her own mouth to him? She never, later, knew.

She had no idea how long they stayed, kissing each other, wordless, one warm throbbing unit of flesh and bone, among the shadows, with only the sound of the rain on the window-panes.

Over his shoulder, she saw a doll, an antique doll in a

yellowed silk wedding dress and veil, on a long shelf of old toys. Finding breath, she murmured, "Playing in the attic on a rainy day . . ."

"Not playing in the attic. The truth is . . ." He kissed her again. "But didn't you know?" Delicious whispering against the surface of her lips.

"Didn't I know what?" whispered back.

From the foot of the attic stairs, Jane called sharply, "Is he there or is he not, Dana?"

With astonishing verbal agility, Nick, dropping his powerfully claiming arms, called back in his everyday, pleasant Nick voice, "Yes, I'm here, putty knife and all. Dana wants to know how old that bridal doll is." He took a handkerchief from his back pocket and swiftly but gently wiped her lips with it and then his own. Dana was sparing with her lipstick, but what there was of it had been well shared with him. "I gather you want me. I'll be right down. After you, Dana."

Dana, anticipating some kind of encounter at which a third party might not be wanted, went quickly downstairs through an invisible haze of rose-color and music.

"You've just been painting the bathroom?" Jane asked, or accused.

His mind informed him in a fast flicker that she never entered her office until nine-thirty, when her own business day started. She would have upon arising have recourse to the bathroom off her bedroom.

"I started painting at, oh, eight or so, and then it began to rain," he said. "I don't know from where, how, when?—but it came to me that when it's raining it's not the best time to paint." Don't explain further; poor strategy. "But you did say you wanted it painted?" Put on a mildly puzzled face.

"Yes, but there were other things—as long as I'm changing the base color." She was a little put out at herself by exhibiting before these rather penetrating eyes an uncharacteristic household pettiness, an anxiety about nothings. Sweep that impression away, immediately. "For instance, I want a fitted beveled sheet of plate glass on both doors. There's a French baker's rack in the window of Valliere's at Third and Sixty-ninth. I want it for a plant stand. But don't pay more than three hundred tops for it. Suppose you get onto these things right away as long as the painting's to be held up."

"All right," Nick said. "I'll just finish the attic window-pane. The rain's coming in and you wouldn't want your floor damaged. Oak. No expense spared in those days."

At close to eleven, the small slim ashy-blond girl, the girl Nick had taken into the garden a week ago, a year ago, appeared again in the reception room.

She was bareheaded, and raincoated in silver leather. She carried a handsome sable-brown Abyssinian cat. She looked Dana squarely over as though to refresh her memory, and then said, "I don't know if he's told you my name. Lottie Garvin."

"No, he hasn't." The girl's hostility was not difficult to sense because she made no attempt whatever to conceal it. Dana chose not to offer her own name in return.

"Where is Nick?" Lottie Garvin asked in a voice which combined at first politeness and command.

"Out, I'm not sure where, errands of some kind."

"Silly damned job," the girl said to her cat, stroking its head. "Errands! Well, I'll wait for him in his room. If it's locked, there'll be extra keys to it somewhere around?"

"I'm not sure that I—" What was the correct stance here? His room was his own place. But was this girl his own . . . what? Her sudden tangle of emotions confused to Dana what should have been a perfectly simple yes or no situation.

The voice turned a little insolent. "Oh, come on. Nick's keeper? I mean—you just work here, don't you? You're not what might be called the housemother?"

She watched Dana's long slow flush. "You needn't be

afraid of breaking new ground in his absence," she said with a smile. "I do know the room, you know, it's somewhat like a second home."

Of course. She could come and go at liberty if she wished—if he wished—up and down the outer basement stairs, at any time of the day or night. Just ring the bell. Hello, Nick, here I am.

Musingly confiding, Lottie Garvin went on, "I did tell him that, if you're stuck here for a year on contract, the least you can do is replace that horrible rag rug with one of your own, you have much prettier ones at your apartment. He did, though, take down that grim old Kerr Eby etching of a World War One battlefield that used to hang over the bed. Valuable, I suppose, but hardly conducive to . . ."

Dana, now quite robbed of her powers of rational judgment, opened her center drawer and took out the duplicate ring of house keys entrusted to her by Jane. She got up and said, "Come along," and walked to the rear of the entrance hall to the door opening on the basement stairs.

Over her shoulder, she said lightly, and infuriated herself by saying it, "I assume that as you're an old friend you won't pocket his cuff links," and produced from her throat a small but reasonable attempt at laughter.

Back at her desk, she took three telephone calls and very carefully noted down their exact time and content, because she found herself curiously unable to function at this, her daily work.

"Yes. Then you can't make it at eleven-thirty Thursday, Mr. Keene?"

Impatiently, "I just told you I couldn't. Now, the week of the seventeenth might be . . ."

"Playing in the attic on a rainy day."

"Not playing in the attic. The truth is . . . But didn't you know?"

Didn't you know about Lottie and me? I suppose I should

have said something about it but right now, right here, with the rain and all, it's so pleasant to . . .

"How about three o'clock on the eighteenth, Mr. Keene?"

"Yes, fine. I'll be there."

L. Crane King, October 18, 3 o'clock. Write it down instantly before it slips or is blown away by the wind.

Jane dictated three letters to her, striding back and forth in her office as she did so. On the outer edge of her own distress, Dana found herself wondering what she was looking so triumphant about. Having gone up earlier to the library for a book to dip into when she was not otherwise occupied, she had not witnessed Agatha Cowan's exit through the reception room.

"That'll do for the letters," Jane said. "Now, an interoffice memo. To Midge."

Memo? When Midge was only, say, a room and a half away? The world continuing to operate slightly off its axis, things reeling a bit, nothing in ordered pattern.

"Dear Midge. No, just Midge, colon." Jane stopped to think a moment. Should she or shouldn't she? But it was a two-edged sword; she could watch Dana's face, Dana's clear expressive face, as she took it down.

"*You are to stop amusing yourself at my husband's expense.*"

What had made Cowan's wife so sure, when up until then Jane had thought Cowan's accusation was a shot in the dark? He had told her about it, of course. Who, if anyone, had told him?

While she was in the middle of dictating the second of her three letters, her mind had been working simultaneously on this shadowy problem. Memory jumped like a trout in a pool, creating drops and ripples of speculation. Midge had been, long ago, Cowan's secretary, at Bodenheim Enterprises. Nothing really to move strongly on, the thinnest of threads, but . . .

"Midge. It has come to my attention that what is called privileged information is being leaked out of Jane Frame, Inc. This is not only deeply distressing but dangerous to all concerned. Rather than discuss this with you first in person open parenthesis you would fly into a flutter and your mind would go blank close parenthesis, I'd like to have you very carefully comb your own conscience and see if you might perhaps unknowingly have dropped an indiscretion."

She stopped and her glance seized and held Dana's face. Any surprise, any guilt there? No. On the contrary. A look of being somewhere deep inside herself, but able, however preoccupied, to use her operating skills, pencil flying over her pad.

"If you find you have any reason to belatedly suspect yourself or indeed anyone here in the house with access to the offices, let us, after your due consideration, discuss it."

There. At one fell swoop, a retaliatory attack upon, and a future warning to, all three of them, Midge, Dana, and Nick; because of course the girl would tell Nick.

If there was no leak, if Cowan and his wife were just guessing, sniping here and there, she would not have alienated Midge in any final way. Midge was after all of great value to her. If innocence declared itself beyond question, she could dismiss the matter with a, "An opening that was for my ears only—with Amtrak—somehow got to Gorham Management Consultants. Oh well, these things happen."

Dana hadn't gotten to the memo but was typing the last of the three letters when she felt something soft against her ankle, under the table desk. She looked down. It was the Abyssinian cat.

At this moment Jane emerged from her office. The cat strolled over to her. Jane, in a startlingly human way, uttered a small shriek. "Whose cat is that? Get it out of here, Dana. I will not have a cat in the house. I am allergic to cats," which she proved with a sneeze.

Dana picked up the cat and was rewarded by a swift clawing of her wrist. She didn't at the time notice it. The girl was still downstairs, then.

At the halfway point on the basement stairs, she paused. Nick's door was suddenly flung open. Lottie Garvin stormed —yes, no other word for it, Dana thought—out and then whirled around six feet or so from the open door, where Nick now stood.

"—and as far as I'm concerned, you can go to hell and stay there." Then she burst into tears.

"Lottie—" He moved toward her. Oh God, let me out of this, Dana prayed. The cat uttered a loud meow and clawed her again.

The two looked upward. There was nothing to do but proceed. Dana walked down the last seven steps. "Your cat. Would you take it, please, and keep it down here. Miss Frame is allergic to cats."

She handed over the struggling Abyssinian to the weeping girl and thought, going swiftly back up the stairs, how difficult it would be to embrace and comfort a girl with a cat in her arms.

CHAPTER 12

After typing Jane's three letters, Dana looked with distaste at her next page of shorthand. The memo. The insulting security-leak memo to Midge.

I am tired of pointless little cruelties, she said to herself. She tore off the sheet of paper, made a ball of it, and threw it into the fire. The fourth of Midge's morning appointments had just left and her door was open. Dana walked in and closed the door behind her.

She announced, "Jane's accusing someone around here of what she calls leaking privileged information. And as there are only three of us to point a finger at, I just thought I'd warn you."

Midge's mouth fell wide open and her hand flew to her throat: a fleeting but unmistakable picture of a woman backed into a terrifying corner. Then she dropped her hand and Dana saw the convulsive motion of neck muscles as she first gasped and then swallowed.

"Oh no," she said. "No."

Reading, in turn, Dana's face, she openly fought for composure and found it. "Ridiculous, of course," she said. "I think that, even for Jane, she's been overdoing. When I get a chance, I'll talk to her about whatever nonsense this is, and at the same time try to get her to take a break. That perfectly charming house on Fire Island going begging—and it ought to be lovely there at this time of the year. You don't look yourself, Dana—surely you're not taking this seriously?"

"I don't take anything in this house seriously," Dana said,

turning to go back to her desk. I sound, she thought, like a rotten kid who's just had its lollypop snatched away or its balloon pricked and popped. The rotten kid felt like yanking on her coat and walking out, and to hell with Jane Frame, Incorporated.

At least for today.

No, don't. A clear broadcast to Nick Quinn: I can't bear it, I cannot bear it here, now, with you.

Just go to lunch, an overindulgently long lunch, with Bill Barnes, and see if she could retrieve that feeling, which had so recently evaporated, that something promising was waiting in the wings for the two of them.

Midge sat very still waiting for her heart to quiet. Don't come in here yet, Jane, until I gather myself together. If I ever can. If it's possible at all. She had a vision of herself being accused in person by her employer. The giveaway trembling and the miserable flushing. The voice, damp with approaching tears, "But how could you think, how could you ever dream that I—?"

I've got to change, something inside her said clearly and defiantly. Not be Midge anymore. Be, at least to herself, Mildred, a woman of secret strengths, of spine, and dignity.

Mildred must be prepared to deal in a final and convincing way with any suspicion of Jane's. She must be prepared to hold the fort, here in this house. To watch and listen. To spy if necessary. And if she was right, if this persecution of Cowan was to go on and on, Mildred must make herself able to do something about it. Able to stop it.

Office procedure called for Midge's taking over receptionist's duties when Dana went to lunch. Why not, instead of cowering here at her own desk, march out to Dana's place and see how Mildred stood up to the winds of exposure and vulnerability?

Her next appointment wasn't until twelve forty-five. It was

a quarter past twelve now. Half an hour of wings-trying. Sitting down at Dana's desk, her eyes went from the crystal bowl of flame and powdery blue anemones to the typed letters lying beside the bowl. No need to proofread them; Dana's transcription and typing were invariably without flaw. All they needed was Jane's signature.

Come on, Mildred. She picked up the letters, walked straight-backed to Jane's door, knocked, and opened it.

Jane, in a manner unlike her dynamic self, was sitting bent forward in one of the ruby brocade chairs, staring into the fire.

"Your signature's wanted on these letters," Midge said. What was that funny feeling inside her rib cage—adrenalin?

"By the way, it's rather glamorous to be considered a security risk, Jane. Shades of the CIA. Just to put your mind at rest, I, categorically, have neither said nor even thought anything indiscreet about my favorite personnel agency. You ought to know me better than that. As for dear Dana and Nick, I'd call them above and beyond suspicion, and I must say you're extraordinarily lucky in that pair. I think you're overtired, that's what it is, and my advice to you is four or five days at Fire Island. The Dow Jones won't really take a beating if you leave the scene for a short spell."

"Do stop chattering, Midge," Jane said impatiently, getting up and going to her desk. "I happened to be concentrating not on just one thing but two things at once." She scribbled her signature on the letters.

One of the two things, or people, she had been concentrating on was Walker North. He must, one way or another, be made to behave. To return. And not with his hands in his pockets but with his arms open, and hungry.

Walker, one of the men who believed packing to be strictly and solely woman's business, sat in the sunlight in a chair by the window drinking café au lait and thinking up an occasional instruction for Candide.

"Don't pack the cheviot, the gray, I'll wear that. And the Peel shoes, the brown." He turned his head to gaze out the window at the towers of Notre Dame. "Too bad to have to leave on such a lovely day."

"But, for a lovely reason, if things work out," Candide said. "Which shirt?"

"The yellow and white stripe—don't forget it takes cuff links. And the cinnamon tie. Dark gray socks."

They had been in Paris just six days after all; or rather six days in Paris for Candide. Walker had spent two days in Zurich, where he had been summoned by a telegram from the mighty pharmaceutical house, Bernher.

Bernher was relatively new, not quite fifteen years old. Having sent gold-gathering tentacles into every country in Europe, it was now ready to expand to—or pounce upon—the United States. A man was wanted to head the entire American operation. A report had reached Bernher's ears that Walker North, formerly of Squibb and most recently of Greave, of the Belding Group, might be worth taking a look at. In the haughty fashion of many organizations, Bernher preferred to hire away those executives already gainfully (and immensely so) employed; but one had heard that this was a matter of a battle of giants, Cowan and North, which put a different complexion on it.

Walker went with at least outward aplomb through six separate interviews over the two days, and one lunch with three of the directors in a private dining room at the Bernher headquarters building. To have, he supposed wryly, his table manners and tastes in food and wines thoroughly checked. Although Bernher was a German-Swiss company, two of the directors conversed in asides in French and Walker edified the table by dropping easily into the language. A man of culture and presence as well as a highly qualified man, was the consensus.

Departing for Paris, he was informed that the field had now narrowed to three, of which he was one. And would he mind, as soon as he returned to New York, making an appointment with the newly selected Bernher psychiatrist in that city. Walker had heard of this Bernher practice in the selection of its executives, a week of one-hour sessions on the couch, and very much disliked the idea. But the plum was large, and heavy, and sweet, and ripe. Yes, indeed he would.

He was also aware that in a job of this magnitude his life and world and background would be discreetly explored. Now was the time, he told himself, to mind his manners. All of them. Including the marital.

Arnim Bernher himself, at the moment in Zambia, would be in New York at the end of the following week and would like to see and greet Mr. North in person. Would he have returned by that time? Yes, Walker said; he planned to leave this coming Tuesday. Under no circumstances would he have added that he was cutting short his stay in Paris now that this unexpected pot was coming to the boil.

On the Air France plane, while Candide was reading her Michael Gilbert paperback, he looked at without reading his own book, "The Collected Poems of W. B. Yeats." Man of culture. For all he knew, they'd ask the housekeeper for a list of the books on his shelves, the suave spies of Bernher.

He wrote a mental paragraph for their dossier: "Currently having an affair with a woman who runs a successful personnel agency. The woman, late forties, of a powerful personality. Former wife of Malcolm Cowan. Has connections with leading firms, national and international. Midnight intimacies, verbal that is? Possibly dangerous, after an evening's drinking."

The paragraph must be erased at once, and in a crisp and final fashion. The next question was, how to go about erasing it. It was a problem in conjuring tricks, making Jane Frame disappear.

The second subject Jane had had in mind, when interrupted by Midge with letters to be signed, was the follow-up to her exhilarating discussion with Agatha Cowan. It had all worked beautifully. The only worry was that the woman might brace up, decide to suffer in silence, and keep the whole thing to herself. Which wasn't allowable; which would have been a waste of one's time and wits.

She went to her telephone, dialed Belding, and asked the operator for Malcolm Cowan. It would be helpful to know if he was or wasn't out of town.

"Mr. Cowan's office, Anne Pence speaking."

"This is Janet Rivers, Nocella Foods. Is Mr. Cowan there?"

"No. He's in Milwaukee and isn't expected back until late tomorrow night. May I take a message?"

"Thanks, no. I'll call back on Thursday morning."

She took a sheet of her ivory-colored Cartier writing paper from a desk drawer and on it wrote, "As proof of my good faith—and because I want it anyway—please return your key to my house immediately." She signed her name, got out an envelope, and on it wrote "Cowan" with the address of the Fifth Avenue condominium. On her engagement pad, for tomorrow, Wednesday, she made a note. Careful; spying eyes around, no matter what Midge said. Although, come to think of it, Midge had sounded convincing. Her pad reminder was, "Have C's flowers delivered at dinnertime."

To project charm and gaiety across a luncheon table when you are feeling that you have lost the very center of yourself on a flight of basement stairs is not the easiest feat to accomplish.

But Dana managed it so well that, after their coffee, Bill Barnes said, "I don't want to let you go yet. A friend of mine is hanging a watercolor show this afternoon in his brother's gallery. He invited me around to help, and said I could reward myself with champagne, he's all stocked up for the opening. I don't have to call my office but I suppose you do, my dear clerical. Say you're sick or at the doctor's or something."

Dana thought it over. Out of character, irresponsible of her. Poor Midge would be commanded to take over her duties. Poor put-upon Midge. But then, she added to herself, I *am*, temporarily, out of character. I'm not sure just for the time being who, exactly, I am. She went to the telephone, got Midge, and said, "Awful of me, but I'm playing hooky this afternoon."

"Enjoy yourself," Midge said, surprising Dana by the lift to her voice. Strange, when a few hours ago she had looked for a moment pole-axed.

At two-thirty, Nick finished mounting the two beveled door mirrors in the bathroom. He went inquiringly into the reception room, where one fire was lit and one fire was out: Dana. In Midge's doorway, he asked, "Where is our trusty girl?"

"Out having some kind of fling, a good idea on a rainy day," Midge said tolerantly. "If Jane wants to know where she is, she's having her annual physical."

"Odd," Nick said thoughtfully.

"Why odd? A very attractive man came around to pick her up for lunch."

The afternoon was dreamlike in its sense of unreality; or was this what a short spell of identity loss felt like? Dana sat on a table, sipping at a glass of champagne when she remembered it was there at her side, watching the two men hang forty or so watercolors. They were very beautiful, mostly still-lifes of flowers, loose and blurred as though seen through mist. She was sorely tempted to buy one but thought that in this giddy state it might be a mistake. It wasn't that she had had all that much to drink, just the one old-fashioned before lunch. But the light reflected from the glassed-over pictures dazzled and bothered her eyes, and she wondered if she could have picked up a fever somewhere since eleven o'clock this morning and now.

At four-thirty she said she thought she'd go home. They were rearranging the whole north wall of the gallery and she wished them luck and went out and got a taxi to the apartment she shared with her friend Paulette Dacre. Not because she was a great believer in sharing living quarters but because with rents being what they were you just couldn't, even on a reasonably good salary, swing it alone. Unless you were prepared to cast yourself into one of the outer boroughs.

Paulette worked at a travel agency and in the manner of this line of business was away a good deal, sampling cities, hotels, resorts, and cruise liners. Which was a help, even though the two of them got on amiably.

She was away now, in Antwerp, and the peace and silence of the pretty apartment on Central Park South were welcome. But, at a little after five, the silence was pierced by the buzzer at the street entrance. She went unwillingly to answer it. Bill, wanting to take up where they had left off?

No. Nick Quinn. "Buzz me in, you renegade," he said.

A minute later he was at the door. He came toward her with his arms open and extended. Dana backed away two feet.

"I'm not good at being one of a select few," she said. "Maybe it's selfish of me, but there it is."

He paused, dropping his arms abruptly. "Neither am I. You, spending our first afternoon with some man—is he here now, by the way?"

"Have you come unannounced to police this apartment?"

"I have come unannounced to get you back from wherever

you went, from me." He looked rather formidable, standing there in the little mirror-walled foyer, searchlight blue eyes examining her. "By one of a select few, I suppose you mean Lottie. Lottie Garvin."

"Yes. She told me your bedroom was like a second home to her. Which, of course, is none of my business, but she did apparently want to make matters clear."

"That wasn't a visit, that was an invasion," Nick said. "I had no idea that before I came back from Third Avenue she had fired several shots from the hip. Am I to stand here in a wet raincoat, on trial, or may I come in and be offered a nice drink of something? From what I can see of it I like your apartment." He took off his coat and slung it over the back of a straight chair.

"Of course. The wing chair's comfortable, and the park in the rain is . . . scotch?"

"Please."

She felt a little dizzy again. The champagne?

"You should be taking down some of our flinty dialogue for your play," she said, trying to find her bearings. What, actually, were they talking about? Was she being scolded for her unwillingness to join a kind of small, informal harem? Don't you know what year this is, Dana, being his point?

"She tore up my play," Nick said calmly. "That was what the fight was about. She read it—uninvited—while she was waiting for me. After all, it was you who let her in."

"And why did she tear it up?"

"She thought there was too much of you in it. And by the way, the dialogue on my side is not intended to be flinty. If you wouldn't be so intent on keeping your distance . . . oh well." He walked swiftly to her, took her in his arms, and kissed her with lingering warmth.

"But . . . how awful." More a gasp than a measured statement.

"What, this? Oh, you mean the play. It wasn't very good,

just a kind of warm-up, I suppose. Although parts of it . . . and I have a carbon. In any case, I've stumbled on a better idea."

"What is it?"

"I will outline it for you in"—he looked at his watch with a smile—"approximately half an hour. I'm sorry I can't say I'll tell you tomorrow morning over our breakfast coffee here, but unfortunately I'm on duty. You can forget the scotch for the moment, it would only get in the way."

Just before he left, he said against her cheek, "Do you feel more one-and-only now, Dana?"

"Yes. Yes."

"You can also collaborate in another matter, as you're a close observer. What I have in mind is a thing—nothing whatever to do with Lottie—about a woman out to destroy a man."

On this he went out the door, showing a sound sense of the use of exit lines.

CHAPTER 13

At five o'clock on Wednesday, Cowan called his wife, from Milwaukee. He said that if things went as he expected he would be home a little after twelve-thirty. "But don't wait up if you're tired. Is everything all right?"

Agatha had not yet made up her mind whether to clear the air for herself, forever; or to treat the Jane Frame incident with the scorn and dignity it deserved, and embalm it in total silence.

She had changed her mind on this decision at least eight times in the past two days. But the telephone was no place for a spontaneous and relieving outburst.

"Everything's, well, fine. Except that Tan has caught some mysterious Oriental flu or grippe so we're short-handed." After a brief hesitation, "I ought to be used to it, but I find myself missing you terribly."

"We'll remedy that in a few hours. Good night until then, darling."

Darling. He was a man of few verbal endearments. Was he trying to compensate for something, with the word?

Would she spend weeks, months, examining every turn of phrase of his, testing its sincerity and truth? Testing him? Oh dear God, Agatha said to herself.

She tried to interest herself in the evening news on television and then worked at reading her book. At seven-thirty, not wanting to face the loneliness of the big dining room, she had a light dinner at the table by the window in her bedroom.

A veal chop, a salad, a glass of white wine should be no problem to ingest.

Rita brought in a letter with her demitasse. "A messenger just delivered this."

Agatha looked at the single word "Cowan" above the address with a sense of unease. "What messenger service?"

"I don't know, just a young boy in a tan uniform."

She supposed she ought to open it. A hand-delivered letter suggested urgency, and as it wasn't addressed to either Cowan in particular she couldn't accuse herself of invading privacies. The handwriting on the face of the envelope was strong, and very black and confident, and she almost knew who the writer was before she read the short message. "As evidence of my good faith . . ."

The words landed with a thud somewhere in the pit of her stomach. Well, there was no longer any question of telling him the whole story. This woman in her singlemindedness, her consistency, might be in the process of shouting her alleged affair with him from the housetops, or the skyscrapers.

Cowan arrived home at the expected hour, tired, wanting a quiet drink and his bed. Agatha's heart gave one tremendous painful thump when his key turned in the lock.

Kissing her, he said, "Sweet of you to have waited up for me, you look nearly as tired as I feel."

"Mal, something a little odd—troublesome—has happened and it just can't wait until morning."

How did you launch on a faithfully rendered report of a matter like this without having it sound like a flat-out accusation? It was not, she discovered, possible. "I know this is madness, I know it's utterly untrue from start to finish" (did she *really*, now, know this?) "but it's only fair that you should know what's being laid at your door."

It was as though someone else was speaking—uncertainly, stumbling along, and she was standing on one side and watching. Would he flush, would he pale, would he cut her short in stunned rage?

He did none of these things. The skin of his face seemed to grow tighter, the bones harder and more prominent, his eyes, the eyes that never left her face, almost frightening in their focused brilliance.

She wished, after her voice stopped, that he would burst visibly into flames of rage, of outrage. She wished the silence would, sometime, end.

At last he spoke. "Have you got her note? Or did you toss it away, which would be consistent with your conviction that this is all a mad invention on her part?"

"No, I kept it to show you." It was in the pocket of her long yellow at-home dress, put on to show that she wanted to look nice, for him, when he returned. She gave it to him with a hand that trembled. His was steady.

After reading it, "I can't, at the moment, trust myself to talk, or even be in the same room with you, or anyone," he said. "I'd better lock myself away. Good night, Agatha."

Still standing in the center of the living room, she heard from the other end of the long broad hall the sound of his bedroom door quietly closing.

And now the accuser is accused, Agatha thought, shocked and sad. She had felt just before he left the room an iciness, not a heat, coming from him. She had never seen him like this before and had no guidelines to follow; but she knew without question that there was only one thing to do right now. Leave him alone.

The rage was indeed there, deep inside Cowan, as powerful or more so than anything he had ever felt. But he was afraid to let it surface, let it out, even though now there was no one to see him in defeat. Or to hear him, like a tree falling. His legs kicked out from under him in a stealthy, savage back-yard attack.

If he let the monster inside him out, it would immediately seek to slash and smash, to damage beyond repair something or someone.

Choked, and seeing in the dresser mirror the dangerous purpling of his face, he went to one of the windows, threw it open, and stood breathing deeply, looking out over an empire, looking out at New York. An empire with room for many emperors; he was one of them.

But, his power confined in chains, and a great smothering gag thrust into his mouth.

What could he do to her, what could he do about her, that wouldn't in the process of retaliation destroy him too? With the full glare of the press on all his comings and goings, all his business and private connections?

She could publicize any written or spoken denial on his part of the concocted affair between them. In today's lexicon, denials were read to mean, "Yes, it's true."

Had any real and lasting harm been done to his marriage? Was there an unmendable rip in the basic fabric? Only time would tell that.

But there wasn't all that much time left, to think how to channel this fury in a workable direction. "You know me," said a ghostly Jane in his ear. "Once I start on something I never give up."

Right now, he had better go back to Agatha and try to begin repair work. If he didn't do that, he would be aiding and abetting Jane Frame in what he could only see was her campaign to tear him to pieces.

He felt a hard edge of something cutting into his palm. Her note, about the key. It occurred to him that he might have a key to the brownstone, somewhere. When the cleaver of divorce separates two people, little things like keys are not always remembered and returned.

He adjusted his face, lifted and dropped his heavy shoulders, and went wearily out to find and soothe and reassure Agatha. If genuine reassurance was possible, that is.

Walker North felt that his idea, conceived on the plane, was machiavellian.

He had considered alternatives. A final, firm, breakup scene with Jane. That's it, my dear, over and out.

He couldn't quite see her saying, "All right, Walker, I understand perfectly. It's been fun." He could, quite clearly, see and hear her raising hell, the echoes going round and round New York and reaching as far as Tarrytown.

He tried to amuse himself with a picture of being caught by Jane on the steps of say the Metropolitan Museum, a Jane with a horsewhip in her hand. But it wasn't very amusing. Jane when angry could be violent.

Go to her ego. Go straight to her ego. How?

Over her breakfast on Thursday morning, Jane sat contemplating with pleasure the probable thunderstorms still circling about the Cowan condominium.

From the open doorway, Nick said, "Some flowers have just arrived for you. Do you want them in your office or up here, or where?" He was carrying an immense white box.

"Put them here on the table so I can see whether they're private or, as it were, business flowers," Jane said. As he waited, she opened the little white envelope. "Jane, I'll be calling you. I'm back in New York. This is by way of advance thanks. Walker."

Nick was startled to see that this formidable warrior of a woman could look for a flash radiantly pink, and female to her fingertips. The flowers were rare and fragile little white branch orchids, on what looked to be three dozen stems. His swift calculation was, about seventy-five dollars' worth.

"Ohhhh . . . in my sitting room, I think. In the two blue Bristol vases."

Walker, who knew that her business day started precisely at nine-thirty, called her at nine-twenty when she had just finished dressing.

"Jane, my dear, I don't know how to thank you. What a silent schemer you are."

"What are you talking about, not my dear, but my darling?"

"The job with Bernher. What I would call shooting the moon. It's not buttoned up yet, won't be for a week or so, but it looks not only good but unbelievable."

"But why are you thanking *me*?"

"All right, be modest. A whisper here, a murmur there, let your cat out of the bag. You have handed me a lovely, early Christmas tree complete with decorations and lights. The job, as well you know, is nothing less than head of their entire U. S. operation they're just about to launch. I will, I think and hope, have reason to be eternally grateful to you, you marvelous woman."

All right, step into the warm scented bath, relax in it. Even though he had made some sort of magnificently flattering mistake.

"When will you thank me in person?"

"That's the point. You'd know Bernher like the back of your hand, of course. My private life will now go under their X ray. And there's that rather awful business of a week's psychiatric sessions, and so on. I can't be seen for some time to have any emotional or physical connection with a businesswoman whose tendrils comb the international air." He had calculated that he could lay it on with a trowel, with Jane. He was right.

"Oh God. Yes. They do set, Bernher, some kind of high moral tone, don't they. I heard Arnim B. has become a born-again Lutheran or something. Morning services in the company chapel, not quite obligatory, but if you want to get ahead you go down on your knees . . . But—" appalled, as it began to hit her. "You mean, not even a telephone call?"

"Possibility of bugged lines. Those around me questioned, and that kind of thing. But for a top-of-the-mountain job, one can grin and bear it. And now I'm off for my first session with Dr. Lauder. Wish me luck. And I wish you now and always the best of everything, not my dear, but my darling. And again, thank you from the bottom of my heart."

It took a little while for the champagne-y feeling to wear off, the almost head-turning praise and gratitude, his wrong but exhilarating conviction that she had been responsible for this great leap.

A little while to grasp the hard cold fact that for a time at least she had lost Walker North.

Her swift intelligence informed her that even if he didn't, after all, get this towering position, he could lay the blame for it on his association with a "businesswoman whose tendrils comb the international air." Okay. End the association.

The entire sequence a result of his having been flung over-night onto the job market by Malcolm Cowan.

CHAPTER 14

Leave no stone unflung.

It was in a roundabout way that Jane remembered the tapestries.

The long-case clock in the hall chimed six o'clock. A closed-in evening, the rain still coming down. Cheerless time to be alone, when you wanted a drink and diversion. She went from her office into the reception room. Midge's door was closed, voices behind it, hers and a man's, both low. Still interviewing, poor Midge, what a bore that she wasn't instantly available to provide the hand that held the other, companionable glass.

The door opened and a stooped defeated-looking man came out, thrusting his arms into his raincoat. Good riddance.

Going into Midge's office, Jane found her threading an embroidery needle. She occasionally resorted to petitpoint between interviews. Jane thought she must have been working on this object—what was it, a cushion cover?—for at least half the year. Two thrushes against a background of dim soft leaves.

"I gather you're expecting yet another. Come upstairs and have a drink with me. It occurs to one, Midge, that if you chose to embroider a macaw or a peacock it might be good for your modest little soul."

Midge knotted the end of her floss. She lifted her clear gaze to Jane. "How, I don't know, *hard* you sound. As I said earlier, you're badly in need of a rest. You don't look yourself, Jane. Your color's poor."

Jane found herself flushing. Direct criticism, sympathetic personal assessment, from this invaluable but decidedly inferior being—!

"All right, but a quick one," Midge added. "There's a John Walpole due at six-twenty." In the sitting room, she stood gazing at the two vases of white orchids. "How perfectly lovely. Did you find a better job than that tiresome old bank for David Rockefeller, and did he send you those?"

Jane tried unsuccessfully to thrust temptation away. "No. Walker North. Because of a transatlantic word or two from me, he's within spitting distance at least of a colossal post with Bernher. The Swiss pharmaceutical house, you know."

"Oh, good. It's nice to see people fall on their feet. You must be very happy."

You must be very happy, Jane amended silently, that Walker has just bowed himself, until some unspecified time, out of your life. Your, come to think of it, lonely life.

Midge downed her mild Canadian Club and water in a hurry. "Off to your Walpoles and thrushes," Jane said.

Thrushes. Macaws. Peacocks. Needlepoint. Tapestries—

One of Jane's accomplishments was—when she demanded it of her mind—the power of total recall.

It had been an evening in March last year, and the occasion was a small dinner party at which the guests of honor had been the president of Denton Tool and Die, and his wife. They were a strait-laced couple from Pittsburgh, and when her last guest to appear had burst into the entrance hall and uttered his clarion greeting, Mrs. Denton's face was something to see.

"Jane! How I long to cool my burning body against your icy flesh."

To which Jane's calm reply was, "It's good to see you again, too, Darius."

Darius Belding was the last of his line, president by choice of Caravan Imports. Jane had always thought him a little amusingly mad, and considered his firm a rather raffish affair. A nice umbrella, Caravan Imports, for picking up anything and everything all over the world, legal or illegal, to turn a dollar. Caravan was, of course, a member of the Belding Group, considered by some other members as a kind of black sheep of the corporate family.

Darius was in his early forties, tall, slender, with a careless tumble of black hair and a long pale face. His eyes were black and glittering, his nose beaked, his presence darkly vivid and in some fashion disturbing to people who lived orderly lives.

A restless roamer, he was seldom in New York. His official residence was on Sutter Street in San Francisco, but he was seldom there either. He had called Jane the week before from Savannah and said he would drop by and drink Pernod with her; and that he had something interesting and new and naughty to take with it, he was sure she'd enjoy joining him in a little spin. Instead, she invited him to dinner. Anyone named Belding, even if slightly odd, would impress the Dentons.

He outstayed her other guests. They were sitting in the library at one o'clock in the morning when Darius looked inquiringly around the room.

"Where are the tapestries?"

"In the vault at the bank. They didn't go with my new picture." She gestured at the large radiant Roy Diebenkorn abstraction over the mantelpiece.

A year or so before their marriage, Cowan had bought the three tapestries from Darius, wanting, Jane realized, to set himself up as a man of visible culture. They depicted scenes from a tournament, with much flaring of horses' nostrils and gleaming of horses' rumps. "I'll give you the job lot for five thousand," Darius had said. "The provenance isn't entirely clear, otherwise it would be ten times that."

At the time of the divorce Cowan had wanted no possessions from the house, in which almost everything had been bought by Jane anyway.

Now Darius, who had been helping himself liberally to his Pernod and pills, doubled over with laughter.

"That's a good place for them, your vault. I swear you have second sight, you sinister woman. A few weeks ago I happened in the way of work to be looking over an Interpol list. You might call it a Stolen and Never Recovered List. Your tapestries turn out to have been lifted, let's see, fifteen or sixteen years ago from a château in France. The owner, Count Something, was a recluse and very few people had ever gotten to see them. For reasons I won't bore you with I thought they might be a little hot when I picked them up. I thought it would be helpful to unload them on Mal before someone came looking through my warehouse in search of possibly stolen goods."

"What's the position now?" Jane asked, fascinated.

"The position is that you are sitting on, owning, an extremely valuable art treasure. If you want to hang them again at some time in the future, and in the unlikely event that someone recognizes them, say they're copies."

"You don't want them back?"

"Christ, no, I'm in enough trouble—almost always— without looking for more."

"Have you told Malcolm about this?"

"No. You and I were friends, remember, long before I knew him. He might be overcome by his conscience and—" Darius suddenly blinked and raked Jane's face with his black eyes. "And you imagined this conversation, it never took place, my love."

"Of course."

Jane found it exciting, intriguing, to be the owner of a very valuable and all-but-unknown treasure. It appealed to her risk-taking nature. Sooner or later, as a kind of private dare, she thought she might rehang them. In the meantime, they stayed in the vault at the Bank of New York.

The police? The FBI? U. S. Customs, as the stolen tapestries could not, she felt sure, have been cleared demurely through Customs? Perhaps it was just as well not to zero in on the correct authority. The effect she wanted to create was that of a woman dismayed and astonished; and wanting to put things right as soon as possible.

The dismayed woman, in a matter of this magnitude, would not fuss around with the local precinct house but go straight to the top. In the morning, she called Police Headquarters. She said she found herself in the possession of stolen goods and whom, please, should she talk to about it?

She found that doing one's civic duty was not all that easy. The male voice, in a screening fashion, asked the nature of the stolen goods. No doubt thinking, Jane told herself, that he might be talking to some kind of nut. She gave her name and address in a forthright manner and said the stolen goods were very probably tapestries of great value, stolen from a château in France sixteen years ago.

"How is it you waited sixteen years to call us?" the man asked.

She explained that they were part of a divorce settlement and that she hadn't known the origin, or been told about it rather, until last night.

She knew well that if she had been some gray-sounding person at some undistinguished or dingy address she would have been summoned in person to Police Headquarters. But a Jane Frame of East Seventy-third Street with an imperious edge to her cultivated voice—

She was switched to another man who identified himself as

Lieutenant John Vanni, and inevitably had to start all over again.

". . . I wasn't told about it until last night."

"Who told you?"

Tricky. Hand Darius Belding over to Cowan with all the rest of the hot potatoes.

"A friend, an art dealer, who stopped by for a drink on his way to catch a plane to, was it England or France? In any case, he had had occasion to go through an Interpol list of missing art objects and thought he recognized my tapestries. Of course, if you're too busy and I know how busy in this city you are . . . and who knows, they may be copies, but . . ."

Sensing the fish, which might after all turn out to be a rewarding catch, on the point of slipping out of the net, Vanni said, "Will you be at your home address all day?"

"Yes. I will be at my desk here, in my personnel agency at the same address, Jane Frame, Incorporated. And you needn't bother with anything like a search warrant or an order of impoundment or whatever it might be called. The tapestries are in my bank vault, and I will be more than happy to hand them over to the proper authorities, if my dealer friend turns out to have been right."

Vanni called Customs and arranged to meet their national import specialist for art and antiques, Gustave Legge, at the Frame brownstone at eleven-thirty. He first had a criminal records check made on the Frame woman. Nothing on her under F. But she could have gone back to her maiden name; she said she had been divorced, but hadn't mentioned her husband's name. An answer to that question lay within reach.

"Cowan," Jane said. "Malcolm Cowan." She did not mention his position but supplied his home and business addresses.

Vanni, who had a ticklish interest in stocks, recognized the name immediately. Big shot. Walk softly.

"Under what circumstances did he acquire these tapestries?"

They were in Jane's sitting room. She had changed her mind about receiving them in her office. She might be otherwise occupied when her policeman arrived. He would probably be a plainclothes man but would in the normal way stop at Dana's desk and present his credentials.

Watching eyes, listening ears, questions later buzzing among the three of them, Midge, Dana, Nick. What was the police department doing at Jane Frame, Incorporated? She might have guessed wrong about an interior leak, but there was no point in taking chances. Mrs. Phillips, busy waxing the mahogany grand piano in the living room, was instructed to take a Lieutenant Vanni upstairs to the sitting room when he arrived, and then to notify her employer.

"He bought them before we were married, I have no idea from whom. He said he'd made a killing on them. He was good at keeping records and things, he might even have kept the bill of sale. But at least he'll be able to tell you where, how, and exactly when he bought them."

"If he thought he'd made a killing—that they were that valuable—why didn't he want them at the time of the divorce?" Vanni asked.

"Oh, you should know about things like that," Jane said. "Clean slate. Fresh start. All that kind of thing."

Vanni, who had been divorced a year ago, did know, painfully, about things like that. He finished his coffee. "Next stop," he said, "your bank."

He chose not to descend on Malcolm Cowan at his place of work. At eight o'clock, he presented himself at the front door of the condominium and told the nice-looking maid who answered the soft mellow chime of the bell that he would like to see Mr. Cowan. Her fascinated gaze dwelt on his open wallet showing his badge card with his photograph and rank.

Cowan had just gotten in and was having a drink in the living room while Agatha bathed and changed for dinner. Even a man of his powerful presence looked a lonely figure in the immense room, with its cushiony islands of sofas and chairs, its fifteen-foot ceilings, and wall of full-length windows hung in stiff ivory-silk taffeta, its formal corner arrangements, on low marble columns, of carnations and roses and stocks, scenting the air.

Vanni, who at thirty-nine was a prudent and worldly man, had told himself in advance, With a man like Cowan, no tricks, no traps, play it absolutely straight.

He refused a drink with regret and took the chair Cowan gestured him into, a bergère upholstered in poppy-red silk across the round marble-topped table from Cowan's own deep chair.

"Your ex-wife, Jane Frame, has in her possession three tapestries which she says you bought before your marriage to her. Our expert from Customs informs us that they are without any question the ones stolen in nineteen sixty-six from the Château Guéret in Haut Vienne, France. He sets their worth at about five hundred thousand dollars." He watched Cowan's face closely. One of the dents under his cheekbones seemed to flicker, or shudder, a little. Perhaps just surprise?

"I'd like to have the circumstances of your purchase of these tapestries in detail."

Cowan in the course of his business life had had terrible moments, frantic moments, in abundance and had learned—almost—how to control his face and manner.

"Jesus Christ," he said. He stared straight back at Vanni and managed a long, stunned exhalation of breath. "And to think that all these years—"

"Think" being the operative word. Think. *Think*. You can't, as president of the Belding Group, come right out and say you bought them from Darius Belding, president of Caravan Imports, for five thousand dollars because Darius was not quite sure of the provenance.

Take a little more time for astonishment.

Don't let his mind veer to Jane, and the tear of her claws in his flesh, or his fragile dam might burst right now.

"But I don't understand. How did this all come to light, this late?"

"Your wife, ex-wife rather, called us this morning to come and take a look, they're in her bank vault. She said a dealer friend had told her he'd seen them on an Interpol list of missing art objects. She is entirely cooperative and anxious to restore them to their proper owner but couldn't be of any help about the actual purchase."

Think.

"I don't imagine I need tell you that when I bought them I had no idea of their, to say the least, murky origin?" It was a relief to speak, with authority, the absolute truth, even if it only ran the length of one sentence.

"I hardly see you as an international thief," Vanni said, meaning to sound neutral and instead sounding flippant. Cowan's eyes on his face, and the sense of great force in and around him in the air, unnerved him a little.

Cowan was pleased to see that his man was now a bit off center. He put a hand to his forehead. "Now, brain, do some work for me. It's a long time ago. I was with Pursloe Communications then. One of their plants was in San Francisco." Another ring of truth to gratify; he had bought these blasted things from Darius in San Francisco.

"I was beginning to make money and I went around, you know how it is with young men, especially aspiring young men descended from plain Scots railroaders—" He paused and allowed himself a reminiscent smile. "I went around trying to collect a background for myself, for my apartment. Vases, Persian rugs, books in good bindings, that kind of thing. I spent all the time I could spare at dealers and in auction rooms. I don't believe in doing things by slow stages, and in a month's time I'd bought, say, one hundred or so different items, so you can see how difficult it is to pin this one down offhand. But as I'd put out five thousand for the tapestries I may have kept a bill of sale, or some kind of record on paper. I'm provided at my office with a very large safe where I keep my personal as well as business records. I'll do a hunt as soon as I can find time tomorrow and get back to you."

This seemed reasonable enough to Vanni. He could hardly see the head of the Belding Group taking to his heels and disappearing. In any case, they had the tapestries. And to be fair Cowan must at any given time have a dozen pressing matters on his mind to get in the way of distant memory.

"One thing, Lieutenant. Will this appear in the press?"

It certainly would, Vanni thought; nice feather in the cap of the Police Department. He said, "Well, a lot of people are involved—the Customs Service, the owners themselves in France, your ex-wife, Interpol . . . But when you come up with your purchase information, you're probably in the clear, we'll take it from there. You wouldn't be the first one to be sold something that turned out to be something else." He got up to go. He was surprised by a feeling of almost physical fear of this controlled man who was now at what he sensed as a high interior boil. "The sooner the better tomorrow, okay? I'll see myself out."

Cowan thought he had to get himself out too, before Agatha could see his face, in which the enraged muscles were taking over. He had about ten minutes before dinner. Time to—what? For a frightening moment his mind went blank. Oh yes, get to his study, fast, close and lock the door.

Thank God Anne Pence was in. "Emergency, Anne," he said. "Get me Darius Belding if it takes you all night. First try his San Francisco number." He gave it to her. "If he isn't home, he probably has a servant or so there. Track him down, here or possibly abroad. Tell him to call me at my apartment no matter what the hour is. It's absolutely vital."

He poured himself half a tumblerful of brandy and drank it in two swallows. He had never before found himself shaking from head to foot. Rage, fear, attacking him, whipping and beating. Did this haze around him mean an approaching faint? Horrible throbbing in his temples, arteries screaming their response.

A wife to be nice to, a wife soon waiting at the table. A wife stabbed deeply by Jane Frame. And still in her manner a little tentative, uncertain, wanting to believe his denials, wanting to believe his arms and his body.

Oh Christ, oh Anne, oh please . . .

Anne did find Darius Belding, after two solid hours of telephoning. He was not at his apartment on Sutter Street but a man who sounded Chinese and said he was Mr. Belding's valet, on being assured of a business emergency of the utmost importance to Mr. Belding, supplied a list of places she could try, with their telephone numbers. Seven or eight names which could be clubs, bars, restaurants. Six names of individuals, men and women. The Museum of the Legion of Honor, at which Mr. Belding might or might not be attending a champagne opening. Many of the numbers she called were, sometimes for as long as ten or fifteen minutes at a time, busy.

On her fourth try at one of the most determinedly busy numbers, that of a Mr. Tracy Chambers on Stockton Street, she got through, asked in a voice now ragged for Darius Belding, and was told, miraculously, to hold the phone.

The telephone rang at a little after ten-thirty. Cowan took the call in his study. In a few brief sentences he explained to Darius the frightful dilemma that not only he but Darius was in.

"Not I, friend, only you," Darius said. "Handing my name over to the police would be tantamount to writing your own resignation, don't you think?" To this Cowan made no answer; none was possible.

"Now let me concentrate for a moment. Yes—you bought the goods in question from a Mr. L. Ching, a dealer on Gold Street here. Unfortunately, his premises were totally destroyed by fire, naturally including all his records, ten years ago. It actually happened, Mal, fact not fiction. As if that wasn't misfortune enough, Mr. Ching toppled over dead of a heart attack six years ago. His only assistant—it was a small family operation—went back to China."

Cowan's hand gripping the receiver was aching, cold, and wet-palmed.

Suppose he hadn't been able to reach Darius.

Suppose, Darius having been reached, he had chosen to reply, Don't involve me, friend, I know nothing whatever about your tapestries.

The newspapers. "Top-bracket business executive purchased stolen tapestries valued at $500,000 for $5,000."

Public joy in the mighty, fallen. If, at Belding, he survived the clamor in the press, a dark question mark would forever hang over his head.

Perhaps he would not have survived at Belding. Ruin, permanent ruin of everything, opening wide for him to fall into.

These freezing contemplations had only occupied seconds. He became aware that Darius was still talking.

Having taken efficient care of the matter in hand, Darius allowed himself to be amused. "I had no idea," he said, "that Jane was so pure in heart."

Cowan couldn't trust himself to add any comment of his own. But he added it mentally.

And that will be enough, now and forever, of Jane Frame.

CHAPTER 15

Coverage in the Sunday *Times* was light, concentrating more on the history and value of the tapestries rather than on the circumstances under which they had turned up after all these years.

Monday the newspapers zeroed in a little more directly. With a mixture of pleasure and sharp pique, Jane read the accounts of how the Château Guéret art treasure had come to light. The police, she read, were following a lead supplied to them by Malcolm Cowan: the San Francisco dealer from whom he had bought the tapestries.

He would certainly not have supplied Darius's name; even bold and up till now invincible Malcolm wouldn't stick his neck out that far.

His color and style and power acted against him in the proliferating attention of the press. It made him a better, bigger story, although in all recountings it was played perfectly straight; it would be all too easy to invite him to bring suit to the tune of millions. His statement was quoted with unembellished accuracy: "I had no idea that they were stolen. I bought them in good faith from what I believed to be a reputable dealer. The police have asked me not to name him for the time being."

The fact that he had left them behind, in his wife's possession, after the divorce, was helpful to him in the flare-up; although there were those who thought it might be a wise idea to dump them on her before eventually the police caught up with the robbery.

Jane thought she came off very well in print, acting swiftly and honorably in going directly to the police and surrendering the tapestries from her bank vault.

The pleasant part of it was that harm had been done to him in the public eye; there was always the faction that would gleefully deny his innocence in the matter. The annoying part was that he might very probably, with his invented dealer, get off the hook with the rest of the world.

She briefly contemplated sending an anonymous letter to the police, naming Darius Belding as the dealer. What a cat among the pigeons that would be. What a delightful, what a hideous mess it would make, in print and in business.

But Darius might, in spite of his pills and his Pernod, remember that he had told her the story late one night. She knew of no one she could say she was afraid of; but Darius Belding gave her pause.

In a flash of cold insight, she thought, He's, in his way, just as ruthless as I am.

Midge, invisibly, put on Mildred for bravery, for the right tone of voice. On her way, on Monday, to her usual late lunch at two o'clock, she knocked on Jane's door and opened it. Jane was on the telephone, but nothing private to cause a tactful retreat.

". . . he's making seventy-five thousand with United. I'd say it would take a hundred thousand to pry him loose, with one of your nice up-front bonus arrangements . . . all right, I'll have him contact you as soon as he gets back from Tokyo."

"Quite an excitement about you in the paper this morning," Midge said when Jane had hung up.

"Yes." Flat and cool.

"I must say, Jane, I do feel a wee bit . . . I don't know. You used to confide in me about things. You don't, anymore." She felt herself going pink with her daring, but that was all right; a Midge-like pink which could be read as indignation.

"My dear Midge, I wasn't all that sure these were really the same tapestries at all. I had to go about it quietly. And I hardly wanted police tramping all over my reception room."

"I am curious . . . such an amazing story . . . who by the way was the dealer who dropped in and told you? Morgan Beverson? I haven't seen Morgan in years, such a nice man."

Jane gave her a strong hard look and then moved her gaze to the french windows. "No. John Latch. I'd met him at a party, and I asked him to stop by for drinks and also to squeeze out of him a free estimate on the grand piano. I've been thinking that I'd rather have its room than its company."

Put things back on an even keel. Mend Midge's hurt feelings.

"Speaking of company, let's do your birthday dinner tonight, just the two of us. Evenings are lonely now, with Walker off the menu for the time being—having to be ready to dash to Zurich at the drop of a hat."

She couldn't, at this juncture, refuse to sit down to dinner with Jane. Her nature urged an outpouring that couldn't be contained. Stop it, *stop* it, leave him alone, how can you . . . ? But she saw with a controlling clarity that she couldn't risk Jane's wrath, and being very possibly ordered out of this office and out of Jane Frame, Incorporated. She had to stay here, on guard for him.

"Oh, all right, lovely," she said.

After her quick light lunch at the Omelet Nook, she went back to her office and opened the Classified Directory to Dealers, Art. There was no John Latch listed. Perhaps he was one of those snobs who preferred to list his premises in the white-paged directory. There were Latches, but none with a dealer address and telephone number. Out-of-town dealer? Hardly, in Jane's world.

She was not so much surprised as quietly chilled. Perhaps heightened perceptions had been at work, suggesting to her at the time that the name was an invention. Jane's eyes swiveling to the window. Window latch. John Latch.

Uncharacteristically careless of her. But she must be feeling, now, triumphantly on top of things. Things having to do with her ever-mounting attack on Malcolm Cowan.

It wasn't Midge but Mildred who sat down at seven-thirty to dinner with Jane. Who drank her wine and ate her roast beef and spaghetti; cheeks pink, eyes bright, chatter produced in quantity. Who, with her demitasse, opened the little ribboned box by her plate to find inside a pair of small round ear-studs with a rather authentic sparkle.

"Yes, diamonds," Jane said, watching her face. "But modest ones, Midge ones."

Midge flushed deeply. "I'll never be able to thank you, Jane," she said.

In a small ring-bound notebook from Woolworth's, Nick wrote, "Mrs. X knows that a painting left behind by her husband after the divorce had been stolen. Maybe innocent over-painting—sunset scene or something—underneath there's a Botticelli. Goes to the police. Hell and high water for Mr. X."

The report on Mr. L. Ching from the San Francisco police was brief. Yes, dead. Yes, premises destroyed by fire in 1972. They had suspected Ching to have been dealing in drugs on the side but had never been able to get anything firm on him. After his death, the investigation was dropped. In any case, small potatoes: he had left approximately $7,000 in his will to an orphanage in China.

Vanni, who at first had been a little disturbed by Cowan's producing the name of a man and a business both of which had vanished from the San Francisco scene, found himself now satisfied. Drugs on the side. Stolen goods. They went together like Mike and Ike.

"Are you sure you want to wear your diamonds, Viola?" Anthony Nocella asked his wife. "Cowan might heist them."

They were dressing for dinner Wednesday evening at the Cowans, the occasion being a social evening with the president of Maggiore Foods, and his wife. Belding was now in the process of acquiring Maggiore.

Viola Nocella giggled. "Tony, you are *too* much." She patted the three-strand diamond choker around her plump white neck. "I'm sure I'd feel it if anyone tinkered with the safety clasp from behind."

"Really, Herbert," Ada Kellyng said, spooning up a grapefruit segment on Thursday morning at breakfast at the Kellyng house in New York on Sutton Place. "One does begin to wonder about the wisdom of your board. First shocking public nudity and now this talk of international thievery. One or the *other* would be bad enough but . . ."

Her husband, just back from a conference in Auckland, New Zealand, had been waiting for this attack on the domestic front. He made a noncommittal "mmm" sound as he ate his oatmeal. In his morning mail there had been a short nasty letter beginning, "I have tried not to believe in the popular theory that all businessmen are crooks, but now I'm brought up short. As a stockholder I demand that you remove Malcolm Cowan from office."

He had torn the letter in half and put it in his pocket. "What's that you tore up?" the watchful Ada asked.

"A request for funds from what I have been told to be a Communist-front organization."

He finished his oatmeal and said mildly, "Now look here, Ada. Cowan is not only enormously able at his job but he is a man of unquestionable integrity. And it's clear that he's perfectly innocent in the matter of the tapestries. Surely you saw that they'd traced the dealer lead and found that the man was dead and his premises before that destroyed by fire? A common enough practice, I believe, in shaky or shady enterprises wanting to collect on insurance."

"Even so," Ada said implacably.

Even so, echoed a little voice at the back of Kellyng's mind. A troublesome business. Poor Cowan, his private life turned inside out in this way. Top men, he thought, sighing aloud, really ought not to have colorful private lives.

Jane was so refreshed and stimulated by the *Time* magazine coverage of the Cowan-Château Guéret story that, although normally moderate in the consumption of alcohol, she allowed herself three quarters of a bottle of Domaine de Chavelier bordeaux with her dinner of filet mignon and blanched asparagus.

After dinner she went upstairs, took a long hot bath, wrapped up in a toweling robe, and went to her pier glass to admire the reflection. She looked so well, so alive, so—was it a little younger?

In a sudden and spontaneous gesture, she hugged herself. The mirrored face smiled back at her.

By now, she thought, I'll bet he's just about ready to kill me.

Put her off her guard by instituting a severe if survivable strike-back. Not bodily dangerous or painful.

On Tuesday morning Cowan summoned to his office Hugo Haight, vice-president and executive chief of personnel for the Belding Group. Conflicts occasionally arose among the members, such as two groups wanting the same man; in these matters a cool decisive voice from on high was needed.

"As of right now," Cowan said to Haight, "no Belding

member is to use Jane Frame as a source of recruitment of personnel."

Haight raised his eyebrows. Did this spring from the brouhaha in the papers, his ex-wife telling tales on him, or implying them? He knew better than to argue with Cowan but he did murmur, "That does, you know, cut us off from a hell of a lot of good people who won't deign to look for a job through anybody else."

"I know. We'll survive. I want you to send out a letter to this effect to all your personnel heads. You'll want some kind of reason, I suppose. Preferably nothing suable. I'll leave that to you. Practices not entirely in line with those of our Group, or some such."

He sat thinking, tapping his fingers lightly on his desk. "At the same time send out a leaking sort of announcement to Perkinson's." Perkinson's was the most faithfully followed and highly regarded of all American business newsletters; it came out weekly and a subscription to it cost one thousand dollars a year. "With much the same information. That way we'll reach many more ears with this cancellation of relationships."

"If they'll print it."

"They will. They can't afford not to know exactly what's going on on every level. While you're at it, send along the message to some of the more gossipy newsletters, you'll know which, and add *Time*, *Newsweek*, and *Fortune* to your list. Also, of course, *Forbes*. And anyone else you can think of. I'd like"—with a glance at his watch—"to see your announcement and publications list by, say, twelve o'clock."

Haight, who was used to the glory of giving uncontestable orders, did not at all enjoy taking them; like the valet being told to have the striped flannel suit pressed by noon. But he said briskly, "Yes, right," and got up and sped away.

CHAPTER 16

On weekends, as originally specified by Jane, Nick's time was his own after three on Saturday. Most weekends he chose to stay in his quarters and work at his typewriter. When he was tempted to partying or night wandering, Mrs. Phillips' husband, Ellery, took over until Monday morning.

During the week, Ellery was employed in the shipping department at Macy's. He was slender and black, with hooded sleepy eyes and a softly courteous manner. As a security man, he had two drawbacks: he was somewhat hard of hearing, and he was easily frightened. But this information had not been offered when Jane arranged for his weekend time as needed at a handsome hourly rate.

He had his own snug in the basement; a comfortable cot, small refrigerator, and double electric hot plate had been installed for him in the little room which had once been the housekeeper's office.

This Saturday, Nick's typewriter failed to charm. Without much trouble, he secured Dana's company for the afternoon and evening, and after that (promisingly, he thought) who could tell? They proposed to wander around the Central Park zoo in the sun, and go on to see Bill Barnes' friend's watercolor show. ("I've forgotten his name, I was thinking about something else—well, you—but I know where the gallery is," Dana said.) After that they would go uptown to a party given by Coley Hays' sister. "Most parties are terrible but hers are good," Nick said. "Groaning buffet, catered, and all that kind of thing. And usually a piano player from whatever private new sin club's the hardest to get into."

He waited until Ellery arrived at two forty-five, reported that everything was quiet and only Miss Frame was in the house, and then went off to his West End Avenue sublet apartment for a short stop. Juvenile of me, he told himself; but it would be nice to get dressed in something pretty good and show Dana that out of his working clothes he could really look perfectly acceptable.

Ellery was sitting at the battered oak desk in the office-snug —a location for repose which he found pleasantly executive— reading the *Gospellers' Weekly*, when through the open door he saw Jane Frame coming down the basement stairs.

"Good afternoon, Ellery. Would you mind checking the hinges on the door to the attic? I think they need oiling."

On Ellery's departure, she drew a black leather glove onto her right hand, selected a key from her brass ring, and unlocked the door of Nick's room. She went to his bedside table, opened the drawer, and took out the little inlaid gun. She checked to see if it was loaded. It was. She put it into her handbag and went back upstairs to her bedroom, where she put the gun in her own bed-table drawer.

Stepping out of the elevator on the fourth floor, she saw Ellery at the top of the wooden stairs shaking oil from a little can into the attic door hinges. "Sounded all right to me," he reported, "but maybe in wet weather or something . . . and a little oil never hurt a hinge. Anything else while I'm up here?"

"Not a thing. Go back and enjoy your paper."

"JANE FRAME GETS THE BUSINESS. OR—WELL, READ ON," said the leading item in the *Paperweight Newsletter*. "According to an announcement from Hugo Haight, Exec VP, Personnel, the Belding Group will no longer use this super bluechip source for personnel recruitment. Reason given: difference in viewpoints. This closes—with a resounding slam—a golden door to any number of our hundred-thousand-and-up types."

Midge's Saturday mail came in at about one-thirty. Today's yield was dreary, but then it usually was. A letter from a scolding aunt in Binghamton, New York, pointing out that it was four months since Midge had paid her a visit, and describing in detail the state of her varicose veins; a bill from B. Altman, another from her dentist, and the newsletter to which Jane had, mysteriously, given her a subscription as a Christmas present. Midge always made herself skim it because she was subject to an uneasy fear that at some point Jane might fire a test question at her to see if she had familiarized herself with the contents of *Paperweight*.

Oh God. What a body blow. Belding was a bellwether, a style-setter in more ways than one. She felt guilty at the first small flash of glee. (Good for you, Malcolm, that's telling her!)

But she was deeply troubled too. She scrambled two eggs and made herself a cup of tea for the late lunch she was used to. She sat down and wrote a long sympathetic cheery letter to her aunt, promising a visit in the very near future. Through her lunch, through her letter, the troubled feeling continued. Jane, of course, got *Paperweight* along with seven other newsletters. Had she read it by now? What would she do? A torch set suddenly alight—in whose or what direction would the flame leap?

I've got to go and see, Midge decided, not being able to sit waiting for some distant, unheard, but terrible explosion. No need to invent an excuse. Her files needed seeing to, and there was never enough time during the week to tidy them from A to Z.

She didn't even think about a bus, but took a taxi uptown. She had her own key to the house; for some reason she thought it would be wise to let herself in very quietly. And not to cry out to the silent air, "Hi! It's me, Midge."

Noiseless in her weekend shoes—comfortable suede on crepe rubber wedges—she went into the reception room. The door to Jane's office was wide open. The office was empty. No Nick in the garden outside the french windows. He must be off today; somehow you felt his presence even in a house as large as this. The big living room on the other side of the hall was empty too. The mahogany grand piano on whose worth "John Latch" was to have given an estimate shimmered rose-bronze beside a long window.

There are some silences that induce not a sense of ordered peace but of sharp apprehension. Ridiculous. Jane was probably out, or in her sitting room reading, or scheming about titanic job switches.

Now then, Mildred, pick up your feet and go on up the stairs. After all, you did come here to see what was, or might be, happening, after the *Paperweight* bombshell.

Climbing slowly, although these marble stairs were never guilty of even the slightest creak, she was nearing the top when she stopped abruptly. Jane's bedroom was to the left of the landing. She could see the closed door from where she stood.

There was a heavy thudding noise from behind the door and then a silvery tinkle of shattered glass.

What had she thrown, at what? She did throw something approximately once a year, not *at* anyone but in uncontrollable rage.

Had she just now looked at *Paperweight?*

Or—suppose she had in some way hurt herself? The last thing, said a small cold voice in Midge's mind, that Jane Frame would do.

Pure instinct sent her down the stairs and without any noise whatever out the front door. She couldn't be seen from above, or not immediately; Jane's bedroom windows looked out on the garden. She hadn't taken off her weekend poncho, dark brown wool with fringed edges. In it she took a brisk walk around the block; the air now in early November was keen. Do another block in the opposite direction, and don't do it at a fast clip.

Arriving back at the house, she unlocked the front door again. She stood in the hall and raised her voice. "Hi! Anybody on deck? It's me, Midge."

Her near-shout did reach Ellery, who came up the basement stairs to check that it was, indeed, Miss Teller. Jane's bedroom door opened above and then from the top of the stairs she said, "Well, worrywart, what now?" She looked white, her face drawn.

"I thought I'd put in an hour or so on my files." And then to prevent any feeling on Jane's part that this zealous employee might have to be asked to stay to dinner, "I'm due downtown at a, heaven help me, poetry-reading cocktail party at five-thirty."

"The Village never gives in, does it," Jane commented without interest. "I'm off for a bathe and a nap. Have some sherry to do your filing with."

All very well; but allowing her to disappear from the scene this way didn't square with her mission of keeping tabs on Jane.

"You're more than welcome to come along to the reading. You could put wax stopples in your ears. The drinks will be good."

"Thanks, no. It's been a hell of a week and I think I'm getting something. A cup of soup in bed and a book for me. Unfortunately, Nick's not here and Ellery can't cook."

Midge hoped guiltily that an only mildly troublesome virus would lay Jane flat for a day or so, putting her out of business physically.

"I'll bring you up hot tea and toast before I go."

"*No!*" A hard and absolute command. "I'll probably be asleep. See you Monday."

She went back into her bedroom and locked the door from the inside; it wasn't yet time for Midge to look upon the shards of smashed mirror scattered over the parquet floor between the wall and the edge of the rug. Four o'clock now; Midge ought to be leaving at five or so. At ten minutes to five, Jane unlocked her door and went into the library which overlooked the street. Midge went down the outside steps at one minute after five and walked west toward Madison Avenue.

Long hours to put in. But it had to be after midnight, say close to one o'clock. Two would be better, an hour of dark deeds. She didn't feel she could possibly wait that long.

Calling Anne Pence yesterday, again as Janet Rivers of Nocella Foods, she had ascertained that Mr. Cowan would be in town this weekend. "Oh good—just a quick question for him, if it comes up, about Maggiore."

"Please, no," Anne said. "He's planning complete rest and quiet this weekend. He had me cancel two dinner parties." Her firm and forbidding caretaking of Cowan couldn't have been more helpful to Jane. Because if he would be in the company of others this weekend, it would just have to be delayed until the next weekend, or the one after that.

She turned her phone off and pressed the button which would switch all calls to her answering service. Later, to anyone who inquired whether she'd been out during the evening, "I was feeling wretched, coming down with something. I'd taken antibiotics and a sleeping pill."

Eight o'clock. Nine. She was feeling at once too excited and too exhausted to summon up any appetite but she went down to the kitchen and opened a can of Fauchon green turtle soup. Observing the kitchen light illumining the back garden, Ellery came up to be sure there was a good reason for the light going on.

She badly wanted a powerful dose of brandy but a policeman, close enough to sniff, might report that the woman had been drinking, you could smell it.

Going back upstairs, she noted the formidable pile of Saturday mail on the pewter tray in the hall. She hesitated, then decided not to distract her mind from this one, this delicately complicated project.

At eleven she got into bed, propped up two pillows, and tried to read her book. Awful if she were to fall asleep, but she thought there was little danger of that. She was so tense she contracted a sharp pain in the calf of her right leg and had to walk around the room to get rid of it.

Five minutes to one was all she could manage. She got out of the bed and studied it. Not particularly untidied but obviously someone had been resting or sleeping in it, under the covers. She removed the top one of the two pillows and placed it beside the other on the double bed. She lay down again, making a dent with her head on the single pillow she used for sleeping. The heavy floor-length brocade curtains, lined in quilted silk for winter warmth, were drawn; the windows all closed.

From the drawer of the bedside table, she took the little gun in her black leather-gloved hand. Now that the time had come, she was perfectly steady. She fired two shots into the scallop-embroidered hem of the case on her sleeping pillow, a third at the headboard, a fourth at the wall just above the headboard.

Good Christ, what a frightful noise, enough to wake the entire East Sixties, Seventies, and Eighties.

Swiftly, she went to the closet and put the gun into its temporary hiding place, in the toe of one of her tall raspberry suede boots.

Then she went to her bedroom door in her nightdress, hair falling into her eyes, and began to scream.

Ellery, stretched out on his cot, was taking forty winks; he had dutifully set his alarm to rouse him at two for a quick tour of the house.

He was jolted awake by what sounded like a car or truck backfiring. Was it near or was it far away, was it outside in the street or from somewhere high up?

What if it wasn't backfiring, what if it was someone with a gun, outside the door of this house, trying to shoot the lock out? Face coldly glossed with sweat, he sat clutching his sheet and blanket to his chest. His terrified eyes flickered around the room for a weapon, protection of some sort, but found nothing more promising than one of his own heavy shoes.

Maybe it was all over, nothing? Just scary New York night noises. Then he seemed to hear a thin high sound, distantly above, repeated over and over. A siren somewhere? A woman —screaming?

Moaning a little to himself, he scrambled off the cot, pulled on his trousers, and picked up the shoe. In his socks, he went up the basement stairs and opened the door into the hall, where the screams hit him with full force. It was Miss Jane up there, screaming her soul out.

The low light on the table in the hall outside the bedroom, always left on all night, showed him her wild contorted face and her hair falling into her eyes.

"Oh Ellery—thank God—call them—call the police—*is there any blood on me?*" She ran a shaking hand through her hair and frantically examined it.

"Call them and tell them what, ma'am?" Ellery asked, himself shaking all over.

"That a man—that he shot at me while I was sleeping— that he tried to kill me—that Malcolm Cowan tried to kill me."

CHAPTER 17

After Ellery had called the nearest police precinct on East Sixty-seventh Street, Jane said, over only slightly quieter breathing, "Stay here while I try to comb my . . . I don't want to be alone—he may still be somewhere in the house."

"Godalmighty," said Ellery.

"Close the door and lock it there on the inside."

Jane went into her large bathroom and picked up the telephone on the little gilt stand beside the tub. Awful hour to call her friend Carrie Pastor, who lived nearby at Park and Seventy-first, but, of course, the awfuller the better.

Running her words together, she cried to a sleepy Carrie, "I was going to do something a bit nutty and ask you to come over right away and stay the night with me, I'm so terrified, still terrified—although the police are on their way and the night security man's here but he hasn't a gun—"

"What the *hell*, Jane!" cried Carrie.

"Malcolm"—pause for a long breath—"tried to kill me. Shoot me. There are bullet holes on the hem of the pillowcase. I was asleep and . . . then two more bullets when I raised my head and screamed. The door to the hall was just a little open and I could see him, even see the light shining in one of his eyes, you know that strange glare of his—" She stopped and drew three more long breaths. "I think I hear the police now."

"I'm coming over," Carrie said. She had two reasons: deep concern for her old friend, and the wildest kind of curiosity. "Give me fifteen minutes."

Jane brushed her hair, making a deliberate botch of it, and washed her face, splashing water and a scurf of soapsuds on the front of her bathrobe. Maintaining evidence of being more or less totally undone was a bore but a clear necessity.

Two large uniformed policemen—later identifying themselves as Sergeants Cahill and Kovalek—were being let into the bedroom by Ellery when she came in from the bathroom. Ellery, seeing her knees sway, helped her toward the bed and she shrieked, "Oh God, no, not there, the bullet holes—" and he led her obediently to her long chair by the window, where she sprawled like a long-legged thrown-down doll.

"Shouldn't one of you search the house?" she asked, eyes almost starting out of her head. "Of course, he'd know the back way out, he'd go down the back stairs and through the kitchen into the garden . . . there's an opening between this house and the next one, where the garden drain runs . . . it leads through to the street. He could easily be home now, he lives only six or seven blocks away—"

"The house is being searched right now," Kovalek said. "And if you'll just—he being who?"

With uncharacteristic backtrackings, ramblings, and self-interruptions on Jane's part, her story was noted down by the police. (It had all happened so quickly that they must excuse her if she got things a bit jumbled up.)

She had read in bed until eleven and then turned off the bedside lamp and soon gone to sleep. She was first half-wakened when the bedroom door opened a foot or so and against the light from the hall she saw a man, a man whom she recognized as her ex-husband, Malcolm Cowan. She had been too frozen with fear to move and the first two bullets hit the edge of the pillowcase right beside her head. She had tried to raise herself and one bullet went into the headboard, just missing her, she thought. She flung herself to one side and reached for the book she had been reading, and threw it at

him as he fired a fourth bullet. "I was screaming all the time
—I think, I'm not sure—or making awful animal noises—"

At the crash of the book against the wall paved with mirror
squares, he had turned his head, and then he ran out the
door.

She gestured at the book lying open on the floor, the dazzle
of shattered mirror pieces strewn as far as four feet out from
the wall.

After a knock a third policeman came into the room.
"House empty, Sergeant. But someone's been drinking coffee
in a small room in the basement—"

Everybody looked at Ellery, perched nervously on the dressing table bench. Ellery felt a cold rush of primal fear. A
generations-old shrinking took his flesh. The obvious color,
the obvious man, to have attempted the murder of a well-off
woman in a splendid house—

He hardly knew what he was saying. "I didn't hear anything—loud noises, yes, but from the street maybe I thought—
and then I heard her screaming and ran up to her."

"For Christ's sake, gentlemen," Jane said sharply, "don't
you think I know my own former husband when I see him
five feet away from me? Ellery, please get me a brandy and
get one for yourself. In the meantime"—to the police—
"shouldn't you be getting onto him as soon as possible?
Cowan. Malcolm Cowan." She gave them the street address,
recognized in her tone of voice a certain hard efficiency, and
retreated to gasping utterance again. ". . . if he dared go
home after . . ."

"Is there any way you can place the time of the shooting
with fair accuracy?"

"Oh God, how on earth . . . Well, I'll try. It's one-twenty
now. Time is so hard to . . . but at a rough guess, a little before one."

"It was eight minutes to one when I went through the hall

and up the stairs," Ellery contributed unexpectedly. "Clocks are things I notice. There's a big tall clock in the hall."

The third policeman applied himself to photographing the bed, and then took close-ups of the four bullet holes. The room blazed doubly with his flash when he turned to photograph the smashed squares in the mirrored wall. He went to the door and with a brush dipped into a jar of gray powder got to work on the doorknob.

"Oh—fingerprints," Jane said. "You won't find any. He had gloves on. I saw them." She shuddered.

Another knock. Carrie. She flew to Jane. "You poor love!" Jane started all over again gabbling explanations at her.

Kovalek, the senior policeman of the group, said, "We're off now. For the moment. I'll leave a man on the door until eight o'clock."

It had been, as Nick promised, a very good party. They didn't leave until after one. At twelve-thirty Nick asked Dana in a purposeful fashion, "Is your roommate back from her travels?"

"I don't know—she seldom lets me know when she's coming home, and if she wanted to, she couldn't have reached me from this afternoon on."

"Mmmm." He spotted Coley perched on the arm of a long sofa that held nine other people. Bending to his friend's ear, he murmured, "I don't suppose you'd like to sleep at the Yale Club tonight? They must miss you there."

Coley, pink with Canadian Club, said without any attempt to lower his voice, "Sorry, old man, your sublet's busy. I have entered upon an arrangement. That's the arrangement, over there by the fireplace. Something, isn't she?"

Dana was six feet away and heard this half of the exchange. She took Nick's hand and led him into a corner. To cover a mysterious and delightful quaking, she said, "I don't know that I like all this searching around for empty beds." To her own amazement, she blushed; or that was what her face felt like.

Nick smiled at her. "It's all very well for two people to go around with their heads in the clouds, but sooner or later one of them has to be practical. Let's finish our drinks and leave."

An ominous sound of music greeted them outside Dana's door. Had she, perhaps, left the radio on? Not that loud.

All the lights were on as they saw when they went into the hall. Paulette emerged from the living room, a very merry Paulette in a red at-home dress.

"Dana dear! As you see, I'm back." Voices came from a corner of the living room hidden from immediate view, party voices. "I met these delightful people on the plane. When we got in in the afternoon we all went to our various beds to sleep and now we're fresh as daisies again. Who's your nice redhead, will he join us?"

"Sorry, I have to go right home," Nick said. "My mother will be waiting up for me. Good night, Dana."

"He looks good-natured but he sounded quite irascible," Paulette said.

Nick took a taxi to the brownstone, went down the outer basement stairs, and let himself in. At the sound of the door opening, Ellery's voice shouted from his bedroom-office, "Who's that? There's a policeman on the door, a policeman in this house and—"

"It's okay, Ellery. Nick."

"Godalmighty." Ellery emerged, still carrying one shoe in his hand. "You're one man I'm glad to see."

"What's the matter?"

Ellery told him what was the matter, interspersing his narrative three times with ". . . bullet holes and broken glass all over the room . . ."

Nick felt shock on two distinctly different levels.

"But she's all right?"

"Yes, a friend of hers came to stay for the night, they've

moved up to the third floor—the police sealed up her bed-room, and who could sleep there anyway where someone tried to kill you?"

Where someone tried to kill you. Who? Why? And—really?

Ellery answered the first unspoken question. "I don't mean someone, I mean the man she used to be married to, a man named Cowan."

Of course.

He bade Ellery good night in a manner which made clear that he was going to sleep while Ellery remained on watch. He went into his room and crossed to the bedside table. He opened the drawer. The drawer was empty. The little gun, Jane's aunt's gun, was gone. And the box of ammunition gone too, bullets being identifiable objects.

CHAPTER 18

Cowan answered the peremptory ringing at the door himself, giving every evidence of a man freshly yanked from deep sleep and extremely annoyed about it.

Entering the living room with him, Kovalek saw a woman standing in an open arch at the far end of it, a tall ghost of a woman in the light of the one lamp burning in that enormous room. She was fumblingly tying the sash of her robe.

He had already identified himself and Cahill to Cowan. He called across the room, "If you're Mrs. Cowan, would you mind going back to—uh—rest or whatever, and then we'd like to talk to you in a few minutes."

Husband and wife testifying for each other; inevitable and, of course, unreliable. But he could at least take her by surprise.

There was no invitation to sit down; the three men stood, Cowan in his foulard robe over bare strong legs. Hadn't had time to put on his pajamas or more probably didn't wear them at all, Kovalek recorded in a mechanical way. He had no firm ideas whatever yet about the goings-on at East Seventy-third Street.

Hell, it would be the simplest thing in the world for his wife, Elaine, to call the police and say he'd tried to kill *her*, and sometimes he felt—well, kidding—but damned tempted. On the other hand, the very real bullet holes . . .

Cowan, as Kovalek had expected, categorically denied the entire business. The one funny thing was, he looked neither stunned, nor outraged, nor like anything a man falsely accused of attempted murder should look. He had his hands jammed into his pockets. His face could have been carved out of stone or marble. His eyes were narrowed and cold.

"Okay." Cahill did the notebook-scribbling, Kovalek the talking. "You say you went to bed at eleven. You'd have servants here who might verify that?"

"The domestic staffs of all the apartments in this building have quarters of their own on the top two floors," Cowan said. "My wife may be able to tell you when they went up. She was still reading in the living room when I went to bed."

"And when did she come to bed?"

"We have separate rooms. I don't know. No doubt she can tell you."

"If you wouldn't mind showing us your bedroom—?"

"This way."

Bed not only very much slept in, but covers lashed as though the occupant had been tossing in a bad dream. Cahill looked around with furtive envy. What a room for a man to have all to himself. How much was that painting over the bed worth? Probably enough for him to retire on, right now.

"Do you own a gun, Mr. Cowan?"

"No."

"You hunt, though? Wildlife, I mean. It seems to me I read somewhere that—"

"Borrowed gear, safer than keeping firearms around the house."

"Well. If you'll show us where your wife's bedroom is?"

Agatha Cowan's room was two doors down the hall from her husband's. There were, between the two rooms, a large bathroom, a dressing room, and a sauna.

Cowan knocked and then opened the door for them.

"Thank you, Mr. Cowan, we'll see your wife alone."

She was sitting in her white robe in a rose velvet chair, hands trying not to clutch the graceful walnut armrests. Cahill, standing near the door, opened his notebook. Even at this distance he felt the cutting edge of worry coming from this woman.

Without any kind of preliminary, Kovalek said, "A woman named Jane Frame has accused your husband of trying to kill her. At about one o'clock this morning."

"Oh no." Words barely audible. Her hands did clutch the chair arms now, long bony desperate-looking hands. She couldn't turn any paler, but her blue eyes widened. She seemed braced against doom.

In her love, in her fear, she did Cowan, for the moment, a good deal of harm.

She read Kovalek's sudden deep frown and put one hand to her mouth trying to still a tremble at a corner of it. Then she tried to gather herself together and think what one said under such circumstances, said to the police about one's husband.

"But he couldn't have. He was here, with me, from—oh . . . twelve until one-thirty or so. So you see he couldn't have. He was right here with me. And in any case"—better to say it late than never—"I never heard of such a ridiculous thing in my life. The woman's a liar down to the bone." A flash of hatred appeared in the transparent eyes. Not dislike, not outrage. Hatred.

"Does your husband own a gun, Mrs. Cowan?"

How, she wondered frantically, had Jane Frame said he tried to kill her? With his bare hands? With a gun?

"No," she said. "No, he does not own a gun."

Did he? She had no idea. She had long sensed, and accepted the fact, that he was a man who had secret pockets in the invisible protective suit he wore.

"You retired at what hour?"

"Eleven-thirty."

"Were any of the servants downstairs to substantiate this?"

"No, they'd all gone up to their own quarters before eleven."

"So it's really just your word against Jane Frame's?"

"Yes. My word and my husband's word. Against Jane Frame's."

What—a thought that tore and stunned—if he had admitted that he had tried to kill her and they were going to take him away, take him to prison? And they were just in some awful way playing with her? She hardly heard Kovalek's, "We may want to talk to you again tomorrow." In hazed disbelief, she watched the two men in their terrifying uniforms walk to the door and leave the room.

Cowan was standing in the hall outside. His immobile presence was disconcerting.

"You won't be leaving town tomorrow, or rather today, Mr. Cowan?" A prudent deference tempered Kovalek's question.

"No."

"Until later, then."

On the sidewalk outside they were joined by Hemp, the third policeman. The doorman, he reported, had not seen Mr. Cowan leaving or entering the building since he came on duty at ten o'clock. "Of course," Hemp added, "ten- or twenty-dollar bills make good blinders." He had also looked into other ingress to the building, the delivery entrance and the ramp to the underground garage. "The trade entrance is chained and padlocked. The garage, no problem, I'd say. There's a night man who'd buzz him in and roll up the doors, but he was as high as a Georgia pine, and probably couldn't remember if it was Henry Kissinger or the Holy Ghost who he buzzed in. He said he hadn't seen anyone since midnight."

Toward dawn Jane woke from an explosive dream ringing with the sound of gunshots.

Was Cowan asleep now or was he striding his floor, shouting vengeance to heaven?

They wouldn't, of course, have arrested him. Not enough to go on yet. Or perhaps ever. If he were some poor unlettered wretch in a soiled shirt, he would have been hauled away handcuffed in the police patrol car for heavy questioning with a blaze of light in his eyes. Or so she was led to believe from her reading of detective novels. The police didn't want open cases on their books, but neatly closed cases. If, that is, she, Jane Frame, could be considered a case. She was after all still very much alive.

But presumably, from the police point of view, you couldn't have women of substance and influence, owners and occupiers of choice Manhattan real estate, subjected to attempted murder in their beds. One way or another, the affair would have to be thoroughly gone into. Questions asked. Other people involved. Word swiftly getting around.

In the next bed, Carrie stirred. She asked tentatively in the darkness, "Jane?"

"Yes, awake, somehow can't sleep . . ."

"I can't either," Carrie said. Liar, Jane thought, having heard whenever she woke Carrie's deep relaxed breathing. "It's five-thirty, if your bedside clock is right. I'm going to run downstairs and make a pot of coffee. Would you like that?"

"Love it."

"Stay where you are. Even if you're not sleeping you *are* resting, poor darling. I'll bring it back up."

Jane didn't stay where she was when Carrie left the room. She went into the bathroom, found a guest pack of cigarettes in the dressing table drawer, and lit one, although it was ten years since she had smoked. Resorting to an old schoolgirl trick, when one had wanted a restful day in the infirmary, she fingered cigarette ash delicately under her eyes. This made her look older, and ill, and, while tearless, shattered.

Carrie was back in ten minutes. They sat drinking their coffee in comfortable armchairs in front of the fireplace. Carrie said, "You do look ghastly. I wonder if . . . perhaps your doctor . . . ?"

"No. All I need is a little time to gather myself up off the floor."

"I was thinking—" Carrie looked into her cup. "Is all this to be kept a secret?"

"Certainly not!" Jane said harshly. "I have no intention of helping him get away with it, cover it up. If Robert had tried to kill *you*, would you just whisper it to your pillowcase?"

Robert had been the first of Carrie's two husbands. She was now married to a wealthy man who was a partner in a Wall Street brokerage house. She herself was a fashionable and successful interior designer and knew everybody; everybody, that is, who was fashionable or profitable to know.

Neither of them ate breakfast; Carrie said she never did and Jane said she couldn't get anything down. Carrie bathed and left the house at quarter of eight. "Are you sure you'll be all right, Jane? I have to dash to lunch in East Hampton, the Harringtons have bought a house there and want me to have it in reasonable shape by Christmas. If you need me again tonight, dear, call me at Eleanor's, we're dining there."

Jane was inwardly amused by her hasty departure. *Can't wait . . .*

There were other places besides courts of law where cases could be tried. Such as, a brunch buffet in East Hampton, or a dining room overlooking Park Avenue.

At ten minutes of eight, Jane, pale and silk-robed, came down the stairs under the gaze of the young policeman sitting in a straight chair near the door.

"Will you please open up your police seal, or lock, on my bedroom for a minute? There's a valuable ring on the dressing table, and I have no idea who may be in and out all day. And there are some warm boots I need this morning."

Acceding to this reasonable request, he watched from the bedroom doorway while she picked up the ring and went to the closet to get a pair of high red suede boots. Funny, though, that a woman who had a few hours ago been shot at and missed death by six or eight inches could be thinking about what footgear she wanted to wear today.

But, women.

Now that the emergency meat-and-potatoes chores had been done and reports duly written by the three men of the 19th Precinct, authority took over in the form of Inspector William Lowe. The names were too big for routine handling; too much money and too much power involved to let it shuffle along as just another piece of daily dirty work.

Lowe was a man in his fifties, well-dressed, gray-haired, and quiet. He thought he would turn his attention first to the two men living off and on in the Frame house, Ellery Phillips and —as supplied by Phillips during a lightning inspection of his basement room in search of a gun—Nicholas Quinn, the all-week maintenance and security man.

Quinn had been reported by Phillips to be out that night. Quinn with, of course, keys to the house. A love affair with the Frame woman; a quarrel? A try at robbery, armed robbery? He'd know what was valuable and have a good idea where she kept it.

As for her own accusation of Cowan, it could have been a cover-up for some man, any man with access to her bedroom. Two birds, in fact, with one stone. Maybe she hated Cowan; divorced wives did not always look back on their former husbands with unimpaired affection. And there had been that business about the tapestries, where it had looked for a short time as though she had landed him in uncomfortably hot water.

No witnesses. Just her word. The word of a highly capable, extremely successful woman of the world.

At ten o'clock on Sunday morning, he arrived at the house after a courteous telephone call arranging this hour. He spent a short time with Jane, partly for a face-to-face assessment of her, partly for necessary domestic information.

Who, he wanted to know, had keys to the house? The locks of the front and rear doors had not been forced or tampered with in any way.

Jane gave him a cool measuring look of her own. "I suppose this is what you call being thorough. I thought I had made myself clear as to who entered this house and tried to kill me."

"Yes, to both. Including being thorough."

She had put on her chalk-striped black suit and made no attempt at makeup but left the gray-lavender blur of ashes under her eyes. She was about to rub one eye to suggest weariness but remembered the ashes just in time.

"There are two cleaning women. Neither has a key. Ellery, Mrs. Phillips' husband, hasn't a key either. Nick Quinn, the all-week man, has one or rather two, the other one to the door of his room in the basement. My assistant, Mildred Teller, and my receptionist, Dana Reeves, have keys. I imagine this is all in aid of trying to pin it on someone else or at least muddy up the waters—Malcolm Cowan being too hot for the New York Police Department to handle?" Lowe left this deliberately insulting question unanswered.

In this town, you no longer wasted time wondering why mates and ex-mates killed each other. They just, with consistency, did. However, Lowe asked, "Can you provide me with any motive on Cowan's part?"

"No . . . except perhaps buried hatred, old vengeances, brought to a boil when the story of those blasted tapestries came out . . . To play devil's advocate, he's under enormous pressure in his job, and this can put a bad dent in people's judgment, or even their everyday sanity. He's always had—or at least in my eight years with him—an ungovernable temper when a raw spot is touched."

Lowe took his leave of her and went off to get his own view of the bedroom. There he found a member of the technical squad delicately digging for bullets in the mattress. "She told me to be careful about this mattress, not to mutilate it, said it came from France," said the technical man.

"Even in great distress," Lowe commented, "a very practical woman."

CHAPTER 19

It was only fair, Nick thought, to give her a chance, give her an out if there was a respectable out.

He found Jane in her sitting room, not reading, not doing anything, just staring fixedly ahead of her. As he came in after knocking, she said, "I thought you were off this . . . calamitous weekend."

"Frightful thing," Nick said vigorously. "Terrible. Are you all right? You look as if you'd been through the wars, but then you have. Ellery told me all about it."

She sighed. He had never heard Jane sigh before. "I'll recover."

"One quick thing. Your aunt's gun is missing from my table drawer." He left this statement unembroidered and its possible relevance to anything at all unexplained.

Jane had thought she would have all sorts of time to cope with this; that it wouldn't come up until some moment in the future when and if Nick bethought himself to open his drawer for some reason. The gun could not under any circumstances be put back, not with four bullets out of it, not with what a laboratory examination would probably document as "recent firing."

She saw now only one way to go.

"Missing from your drawer?" She allowed a bemused expression to drift across her face as though she were really thinking about something else. "Oh . . . it can't be—or perhaps you put it away in another place and forgot about it?"

"No. I didn't."

"Well, do take a good look around, in your room, Nick. I don't really like your not knowing where it is."

A little troubled, but not unduly; innocence itself. Her message was clear: The responsibility for the gun and its whereabouts was handed wholly over to him.

He turned and left the room. Well, Jane, he thought, I did give you your chance. And you gave me your answer.

Jane bent forward, spine tense, a fist clenched on each knee.

She was sorely tempted to fire him out of hand, fire him immediately. "Get out of this house, you disloyal, prying—"

What had he meant by his flat report of the missing gun after he had expressed his sympathies for her? *What had he meant?* His eyes had been disturbing, penetrating, a blue sword of a gaze, seeking, probing.

But no, she couldn't fire him, not yet, not now. He could explain to all and sundry, "I merely asked her about her own gun being missing and that was it."

Drop a word to Lowe, or any other convenient policeman, that since he'd been in her employ things had been missing? A little silver pitcher here, a bracelet there, and that she'd chosen to overlook it because he was so capable and such a good cook? And that he might in his light-fingered way have pawned or stolen the gun outright?

No. Dangerous, with a Nick Quinn. Very.

See it the way it was meant to be seen: that her aunt's little gun had nothing to do with anything and that in any case it had been in the sole charge of Nick. It was momentarily confusing, to be on the inside looking out and on the outside looking in. Maintaining, simultaneously, two separate points of view. What had happened, and what she said had happened.

Like many convincing liars, she found herself half-believing in her narrative. How dare anybody doubt my word? If I said it, it's true.

Restlessly, aware that she was leaving a problem unsolved and perhaps unsolvable, she turned her attention to Midge. What in *hell* to do about Midge?

Of course the story of her perilous night wouldn't make a sound in the press at this stage; nobody would dare play around with allegations when the name in question was Malcolm Cowan.

She could hear Midge: Why didn't you tell me, Jane?

Or, Were you afraid to tell me because you said the man with the gun was Malcolm Cowan?

Let it go until this afternoon. Tell Midge she was too shattered to call, too shattered to even think.

The contributions of two people helped to clear Cowan in the eyes of the police that Sunday. If "clear" was the correct word, Lowe thought, in the shadowy one-sided case against him.

After leaving Jane, he hied himself to the basement, where he had been told he would probably find Nick Quinn.

Nick was there, eating a late breakfast of bacon and eggs. At first glance, Lowe thought he offered an admirable suspect. A well-mannered, attractive man spending his days on the humble chores of house maintenance? Ideal setup for intelligent, planned robbery; and he would make, if you were Jane Frame, a thoroughly acceptable lover into the bargain.

This fancy was put to flight by Nick's producing his whereabouts at the time of the near-crime. "There were about forty people at the party who can vouch for me. Then I took my girl home and we had a nice chat with her roommate at around one o'clock. I stopped for a last drink at the Three Trees down the street—the bartender knows me—and got back here at a quarter of two. Cup of coffee for you, Inspector?"

"Yes, thanks." Under the circumstances, Lowe felt he was free to accept this refreshment.

If Nick could no longer be considered a quick neat answer to the problem, he might be useful in other ways.

"What as a member of the household do you make of all this?" he asked.

Nick met his question with another one. "Is there any real case building up against Cowan?"

"I can't tell you that yet, too many things to fill in."

Lowe was aware of a swift anger rising in the man across the table from him. "I'm off and on working on a play about her—Jane Frame. In the next act, she is going to use her own gun to shoot up her bedroom, then start screaming, then have Ellery call the police. Of course, his name won't be Ellery. In the play. She will announce that her ex-husband tried to kill her."

After a short silence, Lowe lit a cigarette. "Tell me the whole plot of your off-and-on play, from the beginning," he said.

Nick did, starting with the missing gun. It had been there yesterday afternoon when he left the house. He always checked, he said, when he was going to be away for a day or so; guns made him nervous.

The poisonous little *Times* ad; the scene in her office with Agatha Cowan; the provenance of the tapestries discovered by her in such a timely fashion. When his summing-up was finished, he added, "Tales out of school and all that— shameless of me. But from where I sit she's a vicious danger-ous woman and I don't think she should be allowed to get away with anything else in the way of destruction. Frankly, I don't know why Cowan hasn't strangled her with his bare hands. But he seems to have taken it all in stride. I suppose in his job you have to grow a very thick hide."

"An interesting theory, if a bit crazy," Lowe said, after a fur-ther ten-minute exchange with his informant, during which this most unusual woman, Jane Frame, was vividly fleshed out for him. "Her lover who Cowan fired—Walker North—has he been back?"

"No."

"Another log on the fire," Lowe mused. "Speaking of fire, I assume you're prepared to lose your job if I decide to discuss your plot with her?"

Nick said in an undisturbed manner that, yes, he was. "Just for a last act if I ever get to it . . . Well, no, downright curiosity. What would be the police position if you came around to believing this? Would you prosecute?"

"Well, considering . . ." Lowe paused and Nick supplied to himself, seeing who these people are, how big these people are, "probably not. Waste of the public money on private eccentricities. And there is, after all, no *corpus delicti.*"

Jane, aware that the subject of her gun might come up during Lowe's interview with Nick, thought with a sudden ripple of panic, What if he institutes a house search for it, immediately?

She transferred the gun from her boot to her handbag, pulled the boots on, wrapped herself in her lynx coat, and then took it off. Too noticeable. Instead, she chose a plain black cashmere coat.

She remembered seeing an apartment building being demolished on East Seventy-first Street near the river. An eight-minute walk took her there. It was a chilly gray morning, not one to invite New York's Sunday strollers in any great quantity.

On the river side of the building were three dumpsters piled high. Chancy; God knows who might be looking down from nearby buildings. Be quick about it.

She rolled back her coat sleeve and with her gloved hand pushed the gun deep into the soft dusty rubble. Prying eyes might think her one of those peculiar people who, although looking not at all poverty-stricken, poked about in garbage cans and eagerly examined ruined furniture put out for collection by the sanitation department. A protruding end of a brass curtain rod caught her attention. She pulled the rod out, mimed a hopeful study of it, and then in head-shaking rejection cast it back to the top of the heap.

She dusted herself off with, unknowingly, a that's-that look.

Turning to go back, she hesitated. Lowe waiting there, wanting to know where her gun was. Where could she go, for a little while, to escape Lowe's questions?

Nonsense. Face him full-on. "You'll have to keep after Nick Quinn about that. It was in his charge. I haven't seen it since I handed it over to him weeks ago."

Without thinking it out, she found herself heading south. Toward Manhattan House. She felt a desperate need for something, someone of her own. Walker. Indiscreet or not, a few snatched minutes—just a friend on a Sunday walk dropping in on him—might remove this sharp ache of loneliness.

And of fear? Fear of what? Of whom? Malcolm? He couldn't dare to do anything . . . violent . . . to her for what would seem like a second attempt.

She was half a block from Manhattan House when she saw a taxi drive into the curve of the entrance. The far door of the cab opened and Walker got out. For a second she saw his head above the cab roof. Then he bent. Helping someone else out? Yes. Candide. They went up the steps. Candide was laughing about something, head thrown back.

It was getting on for twelve. Denied Walker, she wanted to see and hear a familiar face and voice, to set her feet back into the everyday, normal world. Midge? Yes, see Midge in person, say that what had happened was too appalling to retail over the telephone. Walk all the way down there. It might clear her head of its odd confusion.

At the white building on West Ninth Street, she pressed the buzzer. Silence. Midge must be out.

It was impossible, until she felt better and more collected, to face her glossier friends uptown and go through it all over again, her near-death at Malcolm Cowan's hands.

Damn you anyway, Midge.

There wasn't anybody.

Midge left her apartment twenty-five minutes after Dana's telephone call.

"Nick's here," Dana had said. "He brought a bomb with him and exploded it all over the living room. We thought you ought to hear as soon as possible. Unless Jane's called you?"

"No, she hasn't."

In horrified silence, Midge listened. Dana's report was succinct but thorough. Including the smashed mirror squares on the wall where Jane had thrown a book at whoever was trying —or whoever she *said* was trying—to murder her. She knew the name she would hear before Dana spoke it. "Malcolm Cowan . . . she said.". . . . Talk to him face to face. He might, in a world gone mad, think she was just another mutter of insanity over the telephone. She knew his address. Just take a chance that he would be there. And don't think about any of the consequences. Just think about what must, no question about it any longer, be done.

Waiting in the lobby, she was announced over the sound system, in the Cowan apartment. "Miss Mildred Teller to see Mr. Cowan. She says"—the doorman's tone was incurious—"it's in relation to a brownstone on Seventy-third Street."

Christ, not a reporter, not yet, Cowan thought. There hadn't been a whisper in the newspapers. Teller. Mildred Teller. For some reason amiable and trustworthy syllables? Midge.

"Tell her to come right up," he said.

He was alone in the living room. Agatha, who hadn't slept since her visit from the police, was trying to nap, or close a door on today. When would the first phone call come?

"Agatha, I just heard the most awful thing. Of course it isn't true—?"

At Midge's ring he went to the door and spontaneously—it had been a long time—hugged her. He saw from her eyes that she came as a friend, not as someone bearing threats and trouble. "Come along into the study where we won't be interrupted."

Midge accepted a black leather chair that was too large for her, and a glass of chilled white wine from a dewed silver carafe. Busy man; don't waste his time. How would he be feeling, after this outrageous accusation? She wanted to examine his face but looked quickly away. Something strange about the eyes, the gray sparkle and fire gone out of them.

"I'll make this brief," she said. "I work for Jane Frame—have for eight years. I was the one who sent you that note about the *Times* ad."

"My God, I wondered—"

"I went into the office yesterday, Saturday, to tidy my files. I came in very quietly and I'm sure Jane thought she was alone in the house, except for a sort of watchman down in the basement. I heard her—her bedroom door was closed—throw something, I'm sure against the wall, because I heard the broken pieces of mirror falling on the floor. Later I wanted to bring her tea and toast, she said she wasn't feeling well. But she wouldn't let me into the room. She shouted 'No' at me."

After a short silence, Cowan said, "Setting the stage in advance . . . You know, of course, that I had nothing to do with it."

"Of *course*." What was that funny little sound? Her wineglass, rattling against her front teeth.

"What I thought was that someone, some man, had actually attacked her, and it had occurred to her that it would be great fun to name me. But what you're saying is . . . ?"

"Yes. Otherwise why get one part of the story ready at four o'clock in the afternoon?"

He leaned forward in his chair, eyes intent, lighting up again a little. "Would you be prepared to repeat this information to the police if they're still interested in me?"

"Yes."

He got up, came over to her, and put a hand on her shoulder. "You realize that you're saying farewell to your job. I will guarantee you a spot that suits your capabilities, and whatever you're making now I'll double."

"I wasn't thinking of my job. I couldn't keep it, I couldn't stay there any longer anyway. It's a dangerous house, it's a house full of hate. I'd meant to stand it as long as I could, keeping an eye out for you, but—" Hearing herself, she flushed.

"I don't think that's necessary any longer. She's shot her bolt. After all, what could she do next but kill me outright?"

"Please . . . don't even say that."

"She wouldn't, though. She's left too heavy and hot a trail in my direction. It would be a final bit of self-indulgence she couldn't afford. She'd know it meant down the drain with Jane Frame. Drink up, dear Midge, and we'll have another. At no time did I think I'd end up in court—it's all too flimsy for that. But it's helpful," looking thoughtfully down at his hands, "to have facts at your fingertips."

CHAPTER 20

"I mean, talk about the shots heard round the world," said John Harrington, at the drinks table in the living room of the newly purchased beach house in East Hampton. He was making a pitcherful of bloody marys for the thirsty Harrington guests. There were seventeen of them.

It was the most rewarding gossip of all: the thunderclap kind. Delightfully damaging into the bargain.

The farther the story got from its authentic source, Carrie, the more the entertaining variations.

A metal hair curler had saved Jane's life by deflecting the bullet. Are you serious? Jane Frame in hair curlers? You're, excuse the expression, killing me.

She had chased Malcolm Cowan down Seventy-third Street, shouting and screaming, wearing only her nightgown.

A bomb squad was searching the house. Cowan had figured that there might be some man with Jane—Walker North, you mean?—and had planted the bomb in case he didn't get to use his gun.

I don't believe a word of it. She made it all up. She hates him, you know.

Fired bullets at herself, are you saying? Ten, twelve bullets at *herself*? How?

They say he has a terrible temper when he really lets go.

All in all, it was the most diverting Sunday afternoon and evening in recent memory. Better than a film, and you didn't have to stand in line for it.

As Ada Kellyng could be considered a prime audience on

the other end of the telephone, she was called by three of her friends between four and six o'clock.

Kellyng had gone alone to an afternoon concert at Avery Fisher hall in Lincoln Center, his wife not being a music lover. He came into the Sutton Place house rosy from the walk home in the cold, his head still gloriously ringing with Beethoven.

Ada was waiting for him in the hall.

Kellyng listened to her and then went to the telephone and called Cowan's number. A woman answered, identifying herself as the cook, Mrs. Kramer. "I'm sorry, Mr. and Mrs. Cowan are out of town for the day."

Kellyng could understand, in a surface sort of way over what was deep shock, this fictional or real absence from the scene, and from the insistence of the phone.

All very well to play unavailable on Sunday, but what about Monday? And next week? And next month?

"They say the president of the Belding Group tried to murder his ex-wife."

Whether it was true or false didn't, in the long run, matter. (Unfortunately, Kellyng amended to himself.)

But Cowan seemed to have developed a recent knack for getting himself into scandalous trouble. A phrase kept running rhythmically through Kellyng's head. Once too often, once too often, once too often.

Reluctantly, he decided to call a secret meeting of the board. Tomorrow at the latest. Before this thing got totally out of hand. "Gentlemen, it is my unwilling, indeed painful recommendation to you that . . ."

Dear God.

The lost feeling hit Midge even before she left Malcolm Cowan's apartment.

He was seeing her to the door when Agatha came into the living room. He stopped for introductions. ". . . best secretary I ever had. She's an executive now, as she well deserves. She came to do me an enormous favor, which I'll tell you about shortly." Midge saw a certain pleasure light up his face as he looked at Agatha.

Who had decided that now of all times she must be pulled together, ready to help him with all the strength she could summon. She had bathed and put on an apricot jersey trouser suit, a flattering, skin-warming color for her. She had made up her face with care and for the first time since her visit to Jane Frame, Inc., emanated an inner force and confidence.

Midge sensed some kind of powerful exchange between them, unspoken, close, loving.

"There's no possible way to thank you, Midge dear," he said at the door. "Be in touch, though. And think about where you may want to work, this country, Paris, London, wherever." In ways the light friendly kiss on her temple made it worse.

Well, he's not so badly off, Midge thought in the elevator. He has her. And she has him.

And suddenly, after all these years, I have nobody.

"Paris, London, wherever . . ." ". . . double the salary . . ."

And I have no place.

Lowe's afternoon was busy. What he was beginning to think of as, possibly, the great Frame-Up, was pushed aside for a while for genuine crime: the body of a well-dressed man found in a Cadillac in a parking garage on West Forty-seventh Street.

Returning to his office he found a note asking him to call Malcolm Cowan. He listened to what Cowan had to say and then paid a short visit to Midge.

Why is it so painful a second time, Midge wondered. ". . . I heard her throw something against the wall, and the broken pieces of mirror falling." There was a metallic taste of betrayal in her mouth. Fleetingly, it occurred to her that maybe she was wrong, maybe it was a lamp base, or something else, that had been smashed. And here she was documenting the case against Jane.

"At least I thought at the time it was the mirror tile . . ."

Lowe thanked her, noting that she had been crying. He got a strong impression of kindness and conscience ripped and torn at.

It was insatiable professional curiosity that brought him to the door of the brownstone at six o'clock. He didn't want to waste mental energy wondering for weeks what had actually happened last night, in this house. And a woman who could go to the lengths (if she had) to place the label of murderer on (if he was) an innocent man was a danger that needed dealing with.

He might well be reprimanded from on high for taking verbal liberties with a woman so placed as to be able to make an awful to-do in the press if she chose to. But he could say that he felt it was only his duty to make known to her the opinions of her close associates.

Nick Quinn answered the ring of the doorbell, looking, still in his good off-duty clothing, a most unlikely servitor.

He had found when he woke in the morning a scribble from Ellery taped to the outside of his door. "I'm not coming back to this house tonight. You better stay in tonight. My stomach is bad again."

Not knowing whether or not his views had been passed along by Lowe to Jane, he unlocked the basement door a little nervously. His room looked all right, banishing what had been a small and he told himself ridiculous apprehension; she hadn't taken an ax or set a match to his possessions. He checked the gun drawer: empty. He went upstairs and stood listening in the hall. Lights on in the living room, the hall and, the stairway landing above. There was a noise from the kitchen, a clinking of china.

Jane was pouring freshly made coffee into her cup when he came in. "Taking over for Ellery?" she asked.

"He left me a note. His stomach's bad again. Reading between his lines, I think he was frightened to stay here," Nick reported pleasantly.

"Well, nice to find, in you, such loyalty," Jane said. "In a professional sense, that is. By the way, have you found the gun yet?"

"No."

"Do make a point of a serious search for it, Nick. And right away." She left the kitchen, carrying her cup and saucer without the faintest rattle of Sèvres against Sèvres.

Her composure startled him into the first tiny twinge of doubt. What if, after all . . . ? Interruptingly, the doorbell rang.

"She's probably upstairs in her sitting room," he informed Lowe.

"I know the way, I talked to her there this morning." With an odd tightening of his stomach muscles, Nick watched him go up the marble stairway.

The door wasn't closed. Jane was sitting in the chair by the fire, talking into the telephone. Lowe let the angle of the door conceal him and listened.

". . . yes, I know it's almost impossible to believe, I can still hardly believe it myself. And when you think of it, how appallingly *foolish* of him, considering what it will do to him now . . . yes, he—yes. Of course, it probably didn't occur to him that he might miss. Granted that he did connect—as far as the police and the rest of the world would go it would be just another violent aborted robbery. Not a hint, not a clue, ever, as to who it was. Simply, another dead duck on the upper East Side, where the fortunate people with money live . . . Thanks, no, I'm not in any condition to leave the house. Sweet of you to call, the phone's been going all day, everyone so kind . . . and now good-bye, I must under my doctor's orders take another sedative."

He let a moment or two elapse and then walked in. Jane was sipping her coffee. She said, "Do I gather you have something to report, Inspector?"

"Yes. I have. Some bits and pieces I picked up, which I think you ought to be told about." He closed the door behind him.

Nick, for some reason not wanting to go immediately back to his quarters, went into the darkened reception room and sat at Dana's desk. Well-built as the house was, substantial and close fitting as the doors were, he heard the distant shout which took him back weeks to a sunny morning in October.

"No!"

He got up from the desk and went halfway up the stairs. Lowe had been closeted with Jane for about four minutes. It wasn't hard to guess at what he was communicating to her.

He braced himself against the hysteria exploding now, the weeping, the abandoned screaming.

What would it be like if you really were innocent and were handed this grotesque story about yourself?

The sitting room door was flung savagely open and hit the wall hard. Jane stood in the doorway, her face twisted, wet, and scarlet. Head turned to look back, she shouted, "Get out. Get *out!*" and then either yielded to or produced another storm of sobbing, bent over, hair hanging in her eyes. "How—dare you—"

Lowe got gingerly past her, said, "We'll talk again tomorrow when you've recovered yourself," and took a handkerchief from his breast pocket to wipe his face. He was holding in his hand, Nick noticed, Jane's life-size Steuben crystal apple. He started down the stairs and handed the apple to Nick. "I think she was going to throw it at me," he said. "I thought it would be a good idea to take it away from her. You might see about sedatives." Nick, eyes still on Jane, heard the front door closing behind him.

Not knowing where or how to find words, he started with "Hadn't you better—" and she walked down to him and struck his face with such force that he all but lost his balance and had to grasp the banister.

She was breathing so hard there was a pause between each word. "You sneaking . . . spying . . . bastard. Making up . . . filthy . . . lies . . ." She raised her hand again and he moved down two steps. "Get out of my house, get out of it right now. Go pack your bag, right now, this minute . . ."

Over a heavy beating of his heart, he said, "Should you be left alone when . . ."

Her voice rose again. "I *am* left alone. By you, by Midge— by Midge! Alone. Alone." It was somehow frightful to see that her nose was running but under the circumstances the offer of a handkerchief seemed inappropriate.

"All right. As you say. Right away." Why was he running down the stairs? Because he thought she might launch herself on him from above, release her rage in a crashing fall of bodies?

Twenty minutes later he was on the street in front of the house, bag in hand. He looked up at the tall lighted windows. From the outside, a handsome and spacious city residence, solid, secure. Inside, a house full of hate.

Or despair?

On Sunday nights Midge liked to go to bed early, to be fresh for the week. At seven-thirty she put a packet of frozen creamed chicken into a pot of boiling water, and thought about what she would put on tomorrow morning. Wise to decide this evening, because, sleep or no sleep, Monday morning was always a muddle. The beige tweed suit needed pressing because the last time she had worn it it had rained. Maybe the brown wool—

Then, with a blush there was no one to see, she thought, Midge, you are going right around the bend. You may be locked out of the office tomorrow. You may not work there anymore.

She had waited, minute to minute, hour to long hour, for the blast of the telephone ringing, for Jane shrieking *traitor* at her. But perhaps her disclosure to Cowan hadn't yet reached Jane; perhaps it would be played close to official chests and never would reach her, Cowan now seeming cleared of suspicion.

Or maybe Jane was deliberately torturing her with silence and would be waiting at the door of the brownstone tomorrow when—

Oh dear, what a dilemma. She had foreseen having to resign, but tidily and with dignity. And with the, well, let's say, rosy hope of a new job, arranged by Cowan, ahead of her.

Double the salary. Had she, if you looked at it in a certain light, sold Jane for double her salary? She blushed again to herself and ran a worried hand through her hair. There was a sizzling sound from the stove. The water was boiling over. How long had the package said to heat the chicken? Two minutes, four? The doorbell rang.

Oh God, not Jane come to punish her in person. The eyehole in the door showed her a tan-uniformed man. She let him in and he said, "All-Hours Delivery, ma'am. For you. Just wanted to check that you're home. I'll bring the delivery up."

"Who is it from?"

"Jane Frame, Incorporated."

Returning, he brought in two sizable paper cartons, neatly taped, and set them on the floor inside the door. "There's this note too." He took a white envelope out of his pocket. She went to get change to tip him and felt the note burning her hand as the door closed behind him.

She opened it. The familiar handwriting, forceful, black. "Midge: Good-bye. Jane."

Inside the cartons was a cleaning-out of her office, of every possession she kept there, even things she had forgotten, like a sweater she had brought to work one day two years ago when there was trouble with the oil furnace. Pencils, pens, emergency makeup, two little phials of perfume she had also forgotten, the black rubber boots from the bottom of her closet, a folding umbrella. That was the first box. She left the second box unopened for the moment. More of Midge in it, thrown-out Midge, Judas Midge.

The state of mind that could induce such an act terrified her, more for Jane than for herself. She went to the telephone and dialed Jane's number.

When Jane answered, Midge said, "My parcels have come. Eight years is . . . can't we even *talk*, Jane?"

"No. As I told Nick Quinn—he's been dismissed too—I am now quite alone and intend to stay that way as far as my former associates go." Cold, dead voice. "My note says everything I have to say to you." Line disconnected; empty buzz echoing in Midge's ears.

A surge of her stomach sent her to the bathroom, where she threw up. She washed her face and in a wandering way went to the kitchen. The pot holding the plastic packet of food was still boiling. I'll never be able to eat it, she thought, and—vague—maybe Mrs. Warner's cat in 3E, such a nice cat . . .

When hit by any severe shock Jane immediately summoned brandy. Jane was efficient, and knew how to cope. Perhaps a little brandy, there was a half-full Christmas-present bottle of Grand Marnier on one of her shelves . . . now, where had she . . . ?

There was no need to go to bed early, to be fresh and clear-eyed in the morning. She sat sipping her Grand Marnier and a slow drowsy warmth began to envelop her. Well, the other job . . . it might be nice to work in London, an ocean away from Seventy-third Street . . .

Her phone rang again at eight o'clock. It was Malcolm Cowan. "I've been worrying about you, a bit," he said. "Have there been any repercussions from Jane? As we both know, she can be somewhat dangerous when roused."

"I've been fired," Midge said. "So has Nick—oh, you don't know him—the maintenance man or really, you might say, the security man. I suppose I should worry about her, there all alone in the house. She sounded—in a flat way—like death. Well, all right, I do worry about her, even though . . ."

"Come and see me Wednesday, dear Midge. I'll keep lunch clear for you."

Alone. Alone.

Nonsense. She had friends, lots of them. Look at all those people who had called today.

Called mainly, most of them, because they were dying of curiosity.

She had her work, the fuel and core of her life. The Belding Group blacklisting of her agency might present a small problem for a while. She doubted that it would be a permanent ban. Malcolm, obviously, had instituted it, and there was a very large possibility that Malcolm wouldn't be around Belding very long. Even if the police didn't pursue the matter and bring any kind of charge, the damage had been done. In the corporate world, public image was literally worth its weight in gold. And now he was, if not officially, privately stripped of his epaulets. Privately hardly the word; the telephones, the conversations, the *"have-you-heard's"* had of course been exchanged in a verbal crash from coast to coast. A new picture of him, sketched in sinister black and blazing scarlet, was drawn for the eyes of those at the centers of power.

Well, he said he hadn't tried to kill her. Well, he said he'd bought those tapestries in good faith. But . . . but . . .

But.

The sense of hollowness, of depression, was disturbing. The feeling that now there was nothing left to do, with Malcolm finished. Nothing. Nobody. Just aloneness.

For God's sake, Jane, she chided herself. Nothing left to do? A new staff to be hired; get to work on that tomorrow morning. Dana was a question mark; to any observing eye, having an affair, or having something, with Nick Quinn. Even if she plans to stay, Jane thought, I don't want hostility around me. I want peace, and order, and hard rewarding work. It's high time to turn a corner.

The fire here in her sitting room was burning low, but she was too tired to get up and do anything about it. After all, rather a hectic night, last night, not much sleep. Just rest a bit and regather herself. Then go down to the empty kitchen in the empty house and fix something light to eat.

She closed her eyes and saw again Lowe's calm face, heard again Lowe's calm enraging voice. How he could dare to think, to say, that she—that *she*—

He had said he'd be back tomorrow. He would get nothing but cool denials. No hysterics this time. There wasn't a thing, one way or the other, that he could either prove or disprove. The pivotal evidence, the gun, now in New York's countless throwaway tons, would never be found. He would just have to drop it and get on with more important duties. She had read a little while back that this year's homicide count in the city was up to eighteen hundred or so.

For him as well as for her it would quickly become a thing of the past. Over and done with.

Over and . . . She slept.

CHAPTER 21

He had found his keys to the brownstone a week ago, intact on their ring, in an old red morocco box which held cuff links he didn't wear anymore, and tiepins also out of favor.

Of course, she might have had the locks changed for some reason or another at some time. But if that was the case he could always knock or ring for admittance. He would explain that his visit was very much to their mutual advantage.

When the right time came along, that is.

Was the right time tonight?

After his eight o'clock call to Midge, he told Agatha that he was going to go to his Towers office and tape a speech for the Tuesday night dinner of the American Bankers' Association. "Damned bore, but I'll never get to it during the daytime. Don't wait up for me, I may be late."

His ribs felt as though quicksilver were slipping and sliding about under them and occasionally he felt the need of breathing very deeply to give himself more air.

In his office, he was unable to sit still at the desk but walked the floor, and resumed an inner conversation with himself. Yes, all right, in ways it was a desperate and daring chance to take, but he had been a chance-grabber all his life and this had worked supremely well for him. Besides, there wasn't any real choice. It had to be fast. It had to be now. It had to utilize existing opportunities and facilities. It had to be neat. It had to be simple.

Probate being what it was, the house wouldn't go on sale for months, even a year or more. By that time, this night would be tucked well into the past, people forced to rack their memories but not, naturally enough, sure about every little detail.

He went into the lounge without turning on the lights, lay down on the sofa, and began turning words and phrases over in his mind. After a while, he went back to his desk and began writing on a scratch pad.

The brownstone was about a mile from Belding Towers. Wearing a raincoat and a visored raincap pulled low on his forehead, he started uptown, walking fast, at ten thirty.

History not repeating itself, just actually beginning, he told himself grimly as he slipped through the houses' two-foot-wide aperture with its garden drain, into the back garden. The trees were bare, offering little coverage, but that wasn't a worry. In the city way of living with fear, the curtains and venetian blinds of the windows in houses facing the next street up, their backs to the gardens, were closely concealing right down to the sills. So as not to tempt any vicious secret wanderer with the flash of crystal chandeliers, the gleam of velvet, the sparkle of money.

His key turned in the well-oiled lock and in soft silence under his hand the door opened into the kitchen. No lights on here, but a glow from the hall reached the butler's pantry and relieved the kitchen's darkness. Walk a few paces; listen. Walk several more; listen.

The ticking of the clock in the hall sounded alarmingly loud. He was exposed here. Any door opening above would show him standing near the foot of the stairway, listening again. The living room and what he took to be the offices across the hall from it were in darkness.

A faint, pleasant smell reached his inquiring nose: the air remembering a wood fire. She might after all be out. But that didn't seem in character. She would take care to dramatize her narrow escape from him. Prostrated, under sedatives; the works. Women whose husbands had just tried to kill them didn't go gallivanting around town the following night, not if they were capable of thinking things through. Jane was very capable of thinking things through.

He went up the stairs and to the right of the landing saw a door partly open. Her sitting room. The sweet smell of the dying wood fire was stronger here. She was asleep in her chair, head hanging down and sideways. The book she was reading had fallen on the floor.

He was three feet away from her when her eyes began to open and she lifted her head. She found herself looking straight at the gun in his hand. *Déjà vu?* A dream? She opened her mouth to gasp, or scream, and he said softly, "Quiet, Jane. Quiet. Everything's going to be all right if you do exactly as I tell you."

He moved closer to her and, so that she would get the feel of it, placed the muzzle of the black Smith and Wesson gently on her temple. Holding it there, he looked around the room. She always had a typewriter nearby wherever she was, except in her bedroom. Yes, there it was on a little table-desk set at right angles to the farthest of the three tall windows.

He had thought about having her write by hand, but it might look shaky, or frantic. It might be, to the eyes of those who knew her, a giveaway. And then, the typewriter provided an essential convenience: using the point of a pen, so as not to blur her fingerprints, the last sentence or two could be added to her message. Afterward.

"Go over to your typewriter."

"Get that thing away from my head." Stiffly, eyes raking his face for a clue of what he intended, what he was going to do with her, to her, she backed away from him. He followed, one pace away from her. She went to the far side of the little desk, keeping it between them, still facing him. She removed the typewriter's vinyl cover, and without looking down found the switch to turn on the electric purring.

"Now sit down. Even you can't type, standing, type upside down."

The skin of her whole body was one cold, waiting tingle. She sat down and, not wanting to be humiliated by any further basic commands, took a piece of paper from the drawer and wheeled it in. He was now directly behind her.

"Move where I can see you," she said.

"You're in no position to give orders." He did move a little, where she could see him, and see his gun a foot or so from her head; and where he could read comfortably whatever she was to put down on paper.

"No salutation," he said briskly. "Here we go. 'I might as well begin by saying that I hate Malcolm Cowan.'" She typed in a fumbling way unlike her, fingers rigid, knuckles not wanting to bend. (What did he mean, everything's going to be all right? Is this survival? Or what is it?) No choice, no choice at all except to obey. For the moment.

"'I suppose it started the morning when he said he was sick and tired of me and wanted a divorce.'"

"Why put all that in?" she asked in a sudden flare of reckless defiance. "I was getting tired of you too."

"If this is going to do either of us any good, Jane," he said patiently, "it has to be rounded out. We don't want it to sound as if it was written at gunpoint, do we? That wouldn't get either of us off the hook."

Off the hook. Oh Christ, oh well. She typed the line. His left hand moved and she half-raised herself from her chair. "Don't be nervous. Just referring to some notes." He glanced at a piece of scratch pad paper.

"'I determined that when the right circumstances turned up I would make every attempt to destroy him, in the area of his work, that is. They did turn up. He got to the top of the Belding tree.'" He waited while she got this down and then continued, "'But as his work is his life, destruction one way or another would be total.'"

"This all sounds a bit mad," Jane said in a voice that to her horror shook.

"That's all right. A lot of people do think you're a bit mad and always were. 'I must admit I took a great pleasure even in the little things, personal things, things that having been married to him no one but me would know about. Although the tapestries weren't by any means little things.'"

She took a long breath to try to control her voice, but it still had an upper-register flutter in it. "This missive I suppose goes to Kellyng? Why didn't I start it with, 'Dear Mr. Kellyng?'"

"Let's move on. 'I thought my staging of Malcolm's attempt to murder me was a work of art. Am I losing my grip? The police seem to think I might have had a hand in the thing myself. Of course they'll never be able to prove it, but in a way it's knocked the bottom out of everything.'"

"In some strange fashion, this is beginning to sound like a suicide note."

"No . . . just a thorough paying back, which you more than owe me. Here is your grudging apology: 'I suppose I'm sorry about it all. I suppose hate can turn back on itself.'"

She took her hands from the keys. "That sounds even more like suicide. I won't . . ."

He looked at the gun and then at her temple. "Type it and then sign your name. I don't particularly want to shoot you, Jane, it would make a hell of a noise. Though with the house empty I'd have plenty of time to follow the escape route you sketched out for me last night. No one in his senses would believe a second-go-round, Cowan murdering Frame, or trying to." As an afterthought, "I'd miss your brain, but it would hurt you somewhere, badly."

They were both, although there was no audience to see and applaud, somewhat larger than life at this juncture. Cowan, in the course of doing the most difficult thing of his life, totally in command of his nerves. Jane at the typewriter, spine straight, fingers now darting over the keys, the gun at her head, thinking alternately, "off the hook" and "suicide" and planning a dozen desperate schemes to deal with whatever would happen after the note was finished.

She took a pen and signed it. He took the sheet of paper from her hand. With a conclusive gesture, he put the gun in his raincoat pocket. "Now all we need is an envelope, to be addressed to, let's see, Members of the Belding Board, care of Belding Towers."

With a stunned sense of relief and anticlimax, Jane bent to the second drawer down on her right to get an envelope. Cowan whipped from his inner raincoat pocket a plaid wool muffler and looped it over her head and under her chin. She had time for one terrible scream, one powerful sideways plunge of her body, before the few moments of dying and the moment of death.

She was on the floor now, face down, in final stillness. Cowan wheeled the sheet of paper into the typewriter and under her signature, using the point of the pen she had signed it with, typed, "Now there doesn't seem to be anything else amusing to do." He added a final quote which anyone who knew Jane well would recognize as one that she invariably produced at funerals, from Yeats' inscription on his own tombstone, "Horseman, pass by."

"My conscience is getting in the way of my drink," Nick said to Dana. They had finished a late dinner at Mario's and had gone on to one of his favorite Village bars, dark and comfortable, a talented black man at the piano, a place where hands could quietly hold hands and their two lives conversationally explored at leisure.

"Jane?" Dana asked presciently.

"Do you think there's any remote possibility that a Jane Frame could commit suicide? If you ever saw total wreckage—"

"I very much doubt it," Dana said. "It would be like Christopher Wren destroying St. Paul's."

"You're probably right."

One drink later, he said, "She's standing in your light. I could say I'd come back to return my keys. The only trouble is, I did the proper thing and left them on the tray in the hall."

"I have my front-door key," Dana reminded him. "Conscience being a rare commodity these days, we'll indulge yours. I'll go with you. She might want another woman, not a man, to scream at. Or perhaps to see her into bed with pills."

At Jane's front door, he hesitated. "Perhaps you'd better go up the street to the Three Trees and wait for me."

"No. I like it by your side."

He opened the door quietly and they both stood listening in the hall, just inside the door. A whine, a clank, curiously sinister.

"The elevator," Nick said. "Going down. Stay here."

He went swiftly around a corner at the rear of the hall, just in time to see, through the glass paneling, the roof of the iron-grille cage sliding out of sight at floor level.

At his elbow, Dana whispered, "Maybe she's gone down to inspect your room to see if there's any Nick Quinn left in it. Perhaps she's thinking about fumigation."

"I'll go down. You stay here, and I mean it, Dana." He saw on the hall table Jane's Steuben crystal apple which he had placed there after Lowe handed it to him. He went over and picked it up, he wasn't entirely sure why. It had a reassuring heft.

Dana saw this and suddenly, sharply anxious for him, said, "Wait a minute or so, Nick. She may come right back up. There are old records in the desk in the basement office, she might want to refer to something or other . . ."

The elevator didn't come back up. He gave it two minutes by his watch.

"Go into Midge's office and close the door," he ordered.
"Don't turn any lights on."

Then he opened the door leading down to the basement.
Light came dimly from somewhere. For a moment he
couldn't identify the source. Past his own room, and around a
corner—

It must be the heavy iron door to a further short flight of
steps leading down to the bottom of the elevator shaft, where
the engine housing was. Not liking enclosed small subter-
ranean spaces, he had taken a quick look at it once, weeks
ago, from the top of the stairs. The engine, God only knew
how old it was, was invisible in its great dark iron casing.

He walked silently to within a foot or so of the partly open
iron door. From behind and below it he heard a noise that
was peculiarly terrifying: the sound of panting.

Christ. His hand tightened around the apple. He moved
another two feet and looked down.

Malcolm Cowan was down on one knee. The front flap of
the engine casing was open. Jane was halfway into the box.
One of Cowan's arms was under her waist, the other under
her shoulders. Her head was flopped back. Her eyes were
open. She sent death at him, up the stairs.

Time, the games-player, went on and on.

Cowan looked up to Nick. Nick looked down at Cowan.
Cowan's chest was still heaving. Jane, big tall Jane, would
have been a heavy burden to carry, to maneuver.

Then Cowan's hand went to his raincoat pocket and Nick
saw the gun in it. Nick, with the advantage of being six feet
higher up and the aim of sheer survival, flung the crystal
apple at his head. It struck him over the ear and with a shout
of pain he toppled sideways.

Nick stepped backward and closed the door. The fastening
arrangement was on the outside, a heavy old-fashioned iron
hook and eye, placed above his head, well beyond the reach of
the house's long-ago children.

Even a cornered Bengal tiger—even a Cowan, he thought—couldn't burst open that fastening from the inside. Or certainly not in a matter of minutes. He went to the door of his own room, which he had left unlocked on his departure, snatched up the telephone and called the police, adding in a voice he could hardly recognize, "—and for Christ's sake hurry."

Dana above, in the dark . . .

Could there possibly be another, emergency exit from the bottom of the shaft? What if the Bengal tiger did get out? A tiger with a gun.

He forced himself to go back and stand listening outside the iron door. Silence. Had he knocked Cowan out with the apple? No. A low sound now, a nightmare sound somewhere between gasping and sobbing.

At the next moment the sound was overlaid with the far, then near, and now dying wail of the police siren in front of the house.

"We're both out of work," Dana said the next day. "Will you be my unemployment compensation? I think I ought to get you out of this city for a while. Every street you walk will be Seventy-third Street. Let's go to Italy."

Then, gently, "Nick, darling, you're still off in your terrible thorny thicket. Do come back to me."

He put his arms around her, resting his head in the hollow between her chin and shoulder. His arms tightened. If he listened carefully, he might hear her distant pipers' tunes again. Listen, listen.

Warmth and a beating pulse of love against his body.

After a time, he lifted his head. "I'm back," he said. "Or almost."

"I can't understand it," said Ada Kellyng. "The woman confesses everything and then he kills her. I always thought the man was mad. I suppose you and your board would have swallowed it whole and kept him on. Why, will you please inform me, *did* he kill her? Although a man who . . ." She thought about listing his other transgressions and stopped, seeing the distress on her husband's face.

"Why? I can only assume the letter they found was coerced by him and of course she could deny it all, the next day, so . . ." Kellyng rubbed his eyes. "And if he hadn't been caught in the act, the assumption would have been that she went off somewhere and—and disposed of herself. The Lord knows how long it would have taken to find her—if ever—inside that machinery."

Late Monday afternoon, Anthony Nocella of Nocella Foods called Sigismund Lynas of Lynas Aircraft.

"I had a thought," he said, "about this awful business. Naturally no one of us at the moment is thinking of anything else. What do you say we try to push for Walker North, if Bernher hasn't grabbed him yet? I always thought he was the better man. And," he added, with a flourish that tried to sound mournful, "this is the sad, yes, well, tragic, proof of it."

Mary McMullen, who comes from a family of mystery writers, was awarded the Mystery Writers of America's Best First Mystery Award for her book Strangle Hold. Her other books include Better Off Dead, The Other Shoe, Something of the Night, My Cousin Death, and But Nellie Was So Nice.